ROPER

J. ALSPAUGH

Printed in the United States of America

First Printing 2025

ISBN-13: 978-1-966775-08-9

DEDICATION

To the many editors who have patiently read through my manuscripts over the years and have helped to make each storyline more enjoyable.

Jason Roper Book Series

ONE

He leapt out of the smoking truck and made a run for it.

Jason was out of the police car and after him almost before Mike pulled it to a stop.

The teen was running now, full speed toward the cliffs. Only from the top, in the fading light, the weathered trees and shrubs he was dodging made the gully almost invisible.

"Lord, don't let him go over." Jason pushed himself to go faster. He had to get to the fleeing young man before he reached the hidden edge of the cliff.

Behind him, Jason could hear the eerie wail of sirens as more police cars converged on the scene.

This had started as a routine speeding ticket. Jason's partner Mike clocked the gray pickup going twenty over. With the lights flashing and siren blaring they had closed in for a quick job. Instead, the pickup had swerved back into traffic and led them on a high speed chase right out of town.

They would be a little easier on him because he had kept out of the main traffic areas. Some crooks weave in and out of traffic using the innocent drivers as shields. That is a quick way to lose favor with a cop.

"Stop," Jason shouted. His voice was loud and authoritative, but the young man only picked up speed.

He was less than ten yards from the cliff now, glancing back often. Jason knew he had not seen the edge.

"He's going over." Jason used the radio strapped on his

uniform. "We are going to need an ambulance."

"I've got one on the way," Mike's voice came back through Jason's ear piece.

There was the edge. The kid teetered on the brink, his face registering terror.

Jason lunged for him and managed to grab onto the boy's leg as he went over. It was lucky for him that cliff was hollow at this point. His momentum carried him over. He swung under the overhang but did not strike the rocks that were inches from his head.

Jason grunted with the effort to hold him. Straining against the weight he was gripping, Jason managed to hook the top of his right foot around the base of a scraggly little tree. This gave him a faint sense of stability. Peering over the edge Jason looked down at his captive.

The perpetrator was a young man in his late teens, and Jason was grateful he was of a slender build.

"Help will be here…" A blast of light and sound caught Jason off guard. His hold slipped. The boy's head struck the rock, but he did not fall. Jason clung to his ankle like a lifeline. It took only a split second for Jason register what had happened. The jerk had shot him. Jason had saved his life and the little brat had shot him point blank in the face. Glaring into his captive's wide, startled eyes Jason silently dared him to try again. The only sound was the clatter of the gun as it made its descent into the yawning caverns below.

Blood dripped from a wound hidden by the boy's bleach-blond hair. He stared numbly up at Jason, not seeming to notice his injury.

"That was a dumb thing to do," Jason growled, the irritation evident in his voice. "What would have happened to you if you had killed me?"

The boy continued to stare dumbly.

"Take a look. That little rock you bumped into would not

have done anything to stop your fall. You would have died, Hot Shot. Or at best come up a cripple."

"I shot you in the face."

It was the first time Jason had heard his voice. He adjusted his age estimate to fit the voice of the boy. Seventeen years old, eighteen at the most.

"I shot you," he repeated. A wild look came into his face then faded as his eyes rolled back and his body went limp.

Where are you Mike? Jason wondered. His grip was weakening. The blood from the boy's head ran in a tiny stream down the side of the rock.

"I got them." James Randal's voice came both over the radio and from behind. "Hang on, Jason." It was not over the radio this time.

"Get a rope, Randal," Jason urged. "My hands are slipping."

James met the rescue team and a padded rope was worked into position around the boy's chest. Working carefully they pulled the boy up and onto solid ground, where he was secured to a stretcher.

"Anything I need to know?" the paramedic asked Jason as his team hefted the stretcher and started back toward the ambulance.

"He hit his head pretty hard, Brent. I think it may have knocked something loose."

Brent frowned, "What do you mean?"

"He says he shot me in the face."

Brent looked at Jason as if seeing him for the first time. "There's not a mark on you. I mean there's dirt but not..."

"That's what I mean."

Watching his team carry the boy off Brent shook his head. "Poor kid."

"Yeah." Jason followed him back toward his car.

———

"The defendant says he shot you in the face while he was hanging off the cliff, and then you hit him in the head with a rock. Is this true?"

An amused murmur rippled through the court room.

"Seth hit his head on the rock," Jason answered. "If you look at where we were on the cliff when he went over, you will see that there are no rocks small enough to be lifted. I lost my hold for a second and that is why his head hit the boulder. I did not strike him." Sweat trickled down Jason's neck. He despised courtrooms, and suits.

"So you do admit to having some fault in the wound Seth received to his head."

"It is not a severe..."

"Just answer the question, Mr. Roper," the lawyer interrupted.

"I admit to it as equally as I admit to saving his life," Jason replied adding lawyers to his list of dislikes.

"But it was your own mistake that caused the wound."

"Yes. I already answered that," Jason added the last part in a low mumble.

"Good. As for the gun..." Seth's lawyer looked meaningfully at the jury.

The lawyer talked on about Seth and the gun and how it was found with one shot missing. Jason let his gaze wander over the courtroom. The jury members sat back in their chairs, some doodling, some fidgeting, and some obviously enduring. Seth sat behind a smooth wood table. The wild look Jason had observed at the cliff remained etched in the young man's features. A few officers who were at the scene sat on the other side of the court. Brent and Mike were whispering to one another.

"Mr. Roper, please answer the question."

"Things happened very quickly that day and I can't say that I can accurately retrace the timeline of events. But if

Seth says I shot him, it must have…"

"You did not shoot him." The lawyer was disgusted. "He shot you."

"Oh." Jason looked thoughtful. "Oh, he shot me."

"Yes."

"Where did he shoot me?"

Seth jumped to his feet "In the face you freak!"

"Oh!" Jason acted surprised. "In the face. That's…that is interesting. I have not noticed any extra holes."

A titter among the jury caused the judge to bang her gavel. "Please keep this serious, Mr. Roper. Did he or did he not shoot you in the face." She was obviously bored with the case.

"I mean no disrespect, Your Honor. But Seth hit his head very hard. And to be quite honest I'm not sure how much damage was done…"

"Objection, Your Honor."

"Objection overruled. Please continue, Mr. Roper."

"If I had been shot in the face, wouldn't there be some sort of…evidence in my features? I will agree that he fired the gun, but whether or not he shot my face I will leave up to yourself and the jury to decide. Is it possible that he fired the gun and fantasized about the result?"

"I shot you!" Seth leapt to his feet again. "You are a freak!"

The jury murmured together. As far as they were concerned, the case was closed.

Two

The counselor was waiting on the other side of the thick glass. His face partially hidden by the two-way speaker. He was pretty normal looking. Brown eyes and brown hair that was not dark or light, just brown. He was not wearing the usual business suit and tie. This guy had on a button up shirt and a pair of dark jeans. Seth guessed he was in his thirties.

Seth strode to the glass partition and slumped down in the chair so the counselor could not see his eyes.

"Seth right?"

"You got my file, don't you?" Seth spat back.

"I didn't actually read it," the counselor admitted. "I usually try to get the story from my client before I read someone else's opinion." He wrapped a knuckle on the thick divider. "I was hoping we could meet without all this glass jazz, but the thugs wouldn't go for it."

Seth sat up enough to look over the counselor again. He had been through lots of these meetings, but this guy was cut out of a different kind of cloth. Satisfied, Seth sat back again with a disinterested "So?"

"Do you want to tell me what got you in here?"

"A freak of nature, that's what," Seth muttered.

"That's kinda cool. Two heads or something?"

Again Seth eyed the man through the bullet-proof glass. "You making fun of me?"

"No. Just sorting out the details," he answered calmly.

"They told you I was crazy didn't they." It was a statement not a question.

"Yes." He sat back in the chair and folded his arms. Seth had not noticed before how tall the man was. "But I don't believe everything I hear." He paused before asking, "What made him a freak?"

"I shot him in the face." Seth was getting animated. Behind him the guard shifted to a more alert position. "Right directly in the face."

"That was pretty low."

Seth frowned. Who was this guy?

"Didn't he save you from falling hundreds of feet to your death?" He had not changed his position. "Or worse."

"I didn't want to be saved. I knew it would land me here." Seth was defiant.

The counselor leaned forward. "To shoot a man who saved you is low, but to do it in the face is…" He searched for the word. "That's just sick."

Seth knew the man was right, and it irritated him. "I'm done with this jerk," he told the guard angrily.

"He's not done with you." The guard did not move.

Seth slouched down in the chair and crossed his arms on his chest. His entire body dared the counselor to continue.

The counselor leaned back again, sitting like a relaxed teen instead of a counselor. "So you shot his face, cracked your head, and they called you crazy."

"He didn't die," Seth grumbled. He caught the hint of a frown that flitted across the counselor's face.

"You shot him, in the face, and he didn't die?"

Seth tried to read what the man was thinking, but besides the momentary frown there was nothing else.

"Did you catch his name?"

Seth eyed him for a moment before answering. "They called him 'Mr. Roper' at the trial. He's a freak I tell you. The bullet didn't even phase him. There wasn't a mark on him."

The counselor nodded a little. "So he didn't die, and you think he is a freak. That makes sense."

"Everyone else says I didn't shoot him." Seth was warming up to this man. For the first time someone seemed to believe him.

"Just to clarify, you were hanging by your leg when you shot him?"

"Yes."

"Is it possible that you could have missed since you were shooting at such an odd angle?"

Seth stood up. "It was like this, dummy." He held his hand with the index finger out like the barrel of a gun down by his side. "His head was right there. Like three feet from my gun. Nobody is that bad."

"I still can't believe you shot him point blank."

The counselor seemed more sympathetic to the cop than to Seth, and Seth resented it.

"He deserved it," Seth vented. "I'd do it again in a…"

The counselor rose. "Would you?"

There was something in the counselor's voice that made Seth feel like a little boy who had shamed his father. He was afraid the man would leave, and knew if he did there would be no hope.

"I guess not." Seth didn't meet his eyes.

"You guess?" the counselor pressed.

This guy was tough, but Seth liked him. "I wouldn't do it again." Seth took the chair once more, this time without slouching.

"I work with young men not with sickos." The counselor was brutally direct. "If you are sick enough to shoot someone point blank, you need serious help. But if you are sick enough to do it twice you're headed for the mental ward."

Seth sat quiet, reproved deeply by the blunt statement.

"So, are we going to move forward?" The counselor remained standing, his muscular arms folded once more across his chest.

"Yes." Seth thought it sounded a little too eager. "I guess."

"Good." The counselor put his fists on his hips and looked Seth over once more. "My name's Benjamin. I'll be back tomorrow at ten."

"You are leaving?" Seth glanced at the guard and changed his tone. "Fine. The goon will see that I'm there."

Benjamin watched him go. Seth looked back once and Benjamin raised his hand in farewell. This was going to be an interesting case.

———

"Hello, Miss. Is there an officer by the name of Roper here?" Benjamin leaned his arm on the counter casually. "I am working with the young man who allegedly shot him and was wondering if he would have a moment to visit about what happened."

The secretary pressed the intercom button on her desk. "Is Roper in his office? Someone is here to see him."

Benjamin idly toyed with the beaded pen chain while he waited. It had been almost six years since he had gotten word of his old friend.

The answer came a few moments later. "No, Nancy. Roper is on patrol. Can you take a message?"

Nancy looked up expectantly at Benjamin.

"No message. I'll just try back later. Could you tell me when he gets off?"

Nancy shook her head. "I'm sorry."

"I understand." Benjamin moved away from the counter. "After all, there are creeps out there who stalk officers."

She smiled a little. "Have a nice day."

THREE

"Hello? Anyone home?"

"We're back in the bedroom, Jason," Ellen called.

Jason dropped his duffle bag just inside the door, thought better of it, and stooped to retrieve it. He was tired all the way to his bones.

"Daddy!" Kara, a seven-year-old with bouncing dark hair raced to meet him with five-year-old Benjamin close on her heels. They were talking fast and excited, cutting each other off whenever the other took a breath.

"Ellen dear, could you make some sense of all this?" Jason started toward the bedroom with a child clinging to each leg.

"Drag us, Daddy!" Benjamin squealed with laughter as Jason trudged along.

Ellen met him halfway down the hall. "Levi got his first battle scar." She sounded like she was announcing his first steps. Ellen cut a trim figure in her jeans and t-shirt. On her hip she carried a little boy.

"He scraped his knee." Kara released Jason's right foot and danced around with excitement, not knowing herself why they were rejoicing.

"A real scrape? Like a wound kind of scrape?" Jason dumped the bag once more.

"I wouldn't exactly call it a wound." Ellen turned so Jason could see the little scrape on the grinning baby's knee. "He tried to climb the dishwasher door again.

"Yes Siree, a first class example of a normal child," Jason sighed. "I'm so glad." He put his arm around Ellen's waist.

She looked up at him. "See, all that worrying for nothing."

"He sure took his time getting it."

Ellen laughed, soft and musical. "He's not even one, Jason."

"Almost a whole year without blood can make a man mighty nervous," Jason grinned. Levi held out his pudgy hands and Jason took him.

"Jason Roper! People would think you were crazy to hear you talk," Ellen scolded playfully pushing him away.

"Hey, little Benjamin and Kara both got hurt before six months." Jason lifted Levi up so he could touch the textured ceiling. Levi laughed at the sheer joy of the accomplishment.

"Do me?" Kara and Benjamin begged.

"No." Jason ruffled Benjamin's hair. It was lighter than Kara's. Little Benjamin took more after his mother in appearance. "You two are way too heavy."

"I am glad for you that it happened." Ellen smiled. "I could tell it was weighing on you."

Jason set Levi down and watched him toddle unsteadily to his mother. "I just want a normal kid who can have a normal life." There was more to what he said than his words betrayed.

Ellen caught this and, with an arm around him, steered him back out to the living room.

"Do you want me to heat up some dinner? We had soup."

"I'm too tired to eat, Ellie." Jason flopped on the couch. "I just need to sit down. This was a long day."

Benjamin and Kara clambered up beside Jason and Levi stood by his knee hollering to be picked up.

Laughing, Jason looked up at Ellen. "Maybe I will have some soup."

———

"They are all normal," Jason mumbled to himself throwing his duffle bag into the trunk of the police car. He shut the trunk and got into the driver's seat. "I don't even know what that means."

He remembered his childhood in little snippets of joy or pain. Jason's childhood had been different. He had been coached and trained from the age of three to stand up for the right, even if it was the losing side. His mother had grilled this into him with almost a desperate intensity. Pulling out into traffic, Jason mulled it over. As usual the speed of traffic around him crept downward until he was trapped going five under the speed limit. He was not in uniform but most people slow down when they see a police car, just in case their speedometer is not working. Jason did not mind today, it would give him more time to think.

His father had injected him with 8/15 when he was only three, but until he turned eighteen the formula lay dormant, and his life went on as usual. Jason remembered childhood friends, he remembered the scrapes and bumps it took to learn to ride a bike. He had been a normal child.

Jason sighed. No, he was not normal. Jason remembered when his parents had explained to him how his body would be invincible. He was sitting on his mother's lap. She had looked down at him after his dad had finished explaining, and said very seriously, "Patrick, God designed you to be a hero."

Jason swallowed, even after all the years he missed her terribly.

He remembered the thrill he had felt, and the anticipation over the years. His parents had trained him, pushed him, and required him to become a hero.

"Maybe they have normal bodies, but why should they be normal?" Jason asked aloud. "Why not make them exceptional?"

Looking around, Jason took in the dull sleepy faces of the drivers he was passing. They were normal. They got up, they worked, they partied late or vegged out in front of a screen, and then they went to bed so they could start it all over again. That is not what he wanted for his kids.

He watched a jogger pass him as he waited at the red light. It was a young man about the age of the boy Jason had arrested last week.

Jason's fingers combed through his dark hair. What was he supposed do about the kid who adamantly claimed to have shot him? It was true. The bullet had struck him dead center in the forehead. He had not lied in the courtroom. He had simply left it up to the judgment of the jury. Most people dropped the charges and moved on with their lives, but this kid was different. He did not seem to care if people called him crazy.

Jason eased over into the other lane and turned into the police department driveway. Mike waved at him over the top of his civilian car as Jason pulled into the restricted parking area.

"How's it going, Jason?" he asked once Jason was out of the cruiser.

"Alright. You?" Jason retrieved his duffle.

"You still look tired," Mike observed. "I told you to take that extra day the Chief offered."

Jason laughed, pushing back the heavy tiredness he was feeling. "And miss a day with you? I wouldn't dream of it."

Mike slapped Jason's shoulder. "What would I do without my right hand man?"

FOUR

"Hello, Seth. How are they treating you?" Benjamin strode across the little room offering his hand to the boy.

Seth shook his hand and took the open seat. "How did you arrange this?"

Benjamin shrugged. "I have my ways."

Seth glanced around the little room. A table and two chairs, all of which were bolted to the floor, were the only furniture. "Doesn't look like much fun in here," he observed.

Benjamin's laugh was genuine and Seth liked the sound of it.

"So, where did we leave off?"

"I'm sick and crazy," Seth answered dryly.

Benjamin nodded. "Good, the first step is to realize you have a problem."

Seth made a face. "Yeah, I got caught."

"No." Benjamin pulled a blank paper from his briefcase and laid it on the table. Next he pulled out a little stub of a pencil. "Alright, listen quick. I'm not supposed to have this 'sharp object' in here."

A counselor who broke the rules. Seth leaned forward with interest.

"Okay, you say your problem is here." Benjamin rapidly sketched a little stick figure behind bars in the bottom right corner of the page. "But I want to trace back to what got you here. What was it that set you on this track?"

Seth shrugged.

"Work with me here. Our time is limited." Benjamin drew a line from the top left down to the jailed figure. "What got you here?"

"I dodged the police." Seth watched a neat little car appear with a few rapid movements of the pencil.

"Good, and before that?"

"I robbed a dude."

"Old or young?" Benjamin asked distractedly.

"An old guy's motor home. The job was a cinch."

Benjamin added a little motor home behind the bent stick figure. "Don't get distracted with details. This is an overview."

"Alright." Seth enjoyed watching the counselor draw. He almost forgot it was his life he was telling. "So before that I swiped a car."

"Car or truck."

"It was a truck," Seth answered. "A gray one."

"Good thing it wasn't red," Benjamin observed.

"Why?"

"I don't have red," Benjamin answered absently as he outlined a little Mazda truck.

"You read my file." The truck was a very good likeness.

"Yep." He was shading in the wheels of the truck and didn't look up.

Seth sat back.

"And before the truck?" Benjamin looked up, his pencil poised expectantly.

"You said you wouldn't read it."

"No, I said I hadn't read it. I wanted to meet with you first, and I did. So, what's next?" Benjamin asked adding a few details to the motor home.

Seth could not resist, he sat forward enough to rest his folded arms on the edge of the table and grudgingly continued.

When they were finished there was a whole string of

thefts lined up neatly on either side of the line. They went from the motor home theft all the way back to the first toy he had stolen as a child.

"There you go." Benjamin slid it around so Seth could examine it. "This isn't your problem, this is just the result." Benjamin tapped the jailed stick figure and then slid the pencil back up the line. "All this is your problem. Each time you were tempted you had a choice. Each time you failed you had a choice." Benjamin met Seth's eyes. "You made a lot of wrong choices. You put yourself here. It wasn't the officer, it wasn't the law, it was you."

Seth slouched and glared at the floor. "You are just like the rest of them."

"That was a very vague statement." Benjamin was not phased. "Until you take responsibility for your actions, you will just keep going down this path. Man, you got to look ahead a little. For instance, what if you had killed the officer?"

"I shot him."

"You sound like a broken record," Benjamin replied curtly. He met Seth's angry look without flinching.

"I didn't ask if you shot him. I want you to think a little farther out. If you had killed him, what would have happened?"

"He would have died."

Benjamin rolled his eyes and sat back in his chair. His slouch was almost a mirror image of the young man across from him. "Give the boy a nickel, he's a genius."

Seth waited, but Benjamin said no more.

"Well?" Seth finally asked.

"Well what?"

"Aren't you going to counsel me?" Seth asked sarcastically.

"Be good and keep your nose clean is about as deep as you can go right now." Benjamin was clearly annoyed. "I really thought more of you when I first met you. But now, I'm not sure what to think."

"Hey, this is only our second meeting."

"This is our third," Benjamin corrected. "You missed the last one because you decided to pick a fight with the other boys. I was here waiting."

For the second time Seth felt the weight of disappointment. "Okay, I would have gone to prison," Seth blurted.

"Yes, but more importantly, Seth, you would have lost your freedom forever."

They regarded each other silently.

"You played this game and got away with it. But I've got a little news for you." Benjamin reached out a long arm and pushed the paper toward Seth. "It's not a game."

FIVE

Bullets ricocheted off the wall, raining fragments of brick down on them.

"We've got to get around him." Mike ducked another spray of tiny debris. "He has us pegged like sitting ducks. Where is the backup we called for?"

"I'll stop him." Jason stood, but Mike grabbed his arm and pulled him back down. "Mike, if we don't stop him before the backup gets here, he'll just have more targets to aim at."

Mike gave in. "Okay, but be careful."

Jason grinned. "When am I not?"

Mike rose enough to fire two quick shots then dove for cover once more.

Jason wove his way through the alley to the back door of the bank. He was grateful the thief was dumb enough to leave the door unlocked. This one would be a cinch. Crouched, but moving steadily forward, Jason closed the distance between the desk and the door. The man's full attention was on the little alley where Mike still crouched out of sight. His gun clicked and he fumbled with an extra clip. One quick sprint and Jason was on him. His momentum knocked the robber off balance.

As the man fell, he twisted and sent a bullet Jason's way. Jason jerked the gun from his hand, irritated by the new bullet hole just under his badge. Intent on escaping, the thief did not realize his bullet had hit its mark. This is what Jason had been counting on.

Jason slammed the thief once against the floor to knock the fight out of him. After that, he cooperated as Jason rolled him and slapped on the cuffs. Jerking him to his feet Jason performed a quick pat down before propelling him toward the main door of the bank. Pausing just inside the doors, Jason deftly moved his badge to cover the bullet hole the crook had put in his uniform. At least it was an easy fix this time. Unlocking the front doors he radioed for a cease fire before bringing the man out to meet his fate.

Jason saw the camera an instant before it flashed. It was just enough time to jerk the thief in front of him. How did the press get in so close?

The second flash caught only the palm of Jason's hand as he wrenched the camera out of the startled man's grasp. "Get rid of this guy," Jason growled into his radio.

"Give me my camera." The would-be reporter was slightly plump and probably coddled most of his life.

Jason decided to go easy on him. "Listen, Bud. You are past the secure police line. You don't have a pass, and you are interfering with an…"

Jason did not get to finish. He felt, more than saw the thief jerk beside him. Knocking the press man to the ground, Jason pulled the thief down beside him and froze. The officers coming to deal with the camera man followed Jason's lead.

"What is it, Jason?" Mike's voice crackled in Jason's ear.

Removing the ear piece Jason listened hard, scanning first the ground level and then the rooftops. Nothing. Jason pushed himself up enough to roll the crook onto his back. In the pulsing lights of the cruisers, Jason saw the unmistakable stain of blood spreading from the wound in the man's chest. He knew instantly that the man was dead.

Replacing his ear piece Jason let the other officers know what had happened. They pulled out, keeping low to the ground. The medics would deal with the body.

Jason put the blubbering press man in the back of a cruiser and closed the door.

"What got him?" It seemed to be the question of the night, but Mike was asking it now.

"I don't know, Mike." Jason ran his fingers through his hair. "I just felt him jerk. I didn't hear anything."

Mike frowned. "Why would someone shoot him?"

"I don't know."

Together they scanned the rooftops once more. Jason was careful to stand just slightly in front of Mike in case he needed to shield his friend.

"I don't see anything unusual." Mike finally said.

"You go ahead and head back to the office, I need a little time."

"Translated: I am going to go snoop around." Mike shook his head. "If the Chief knew what you really do on the job, he would fire me for letting you."

"Then don't tell him." Jason was not in the mood for jokes. Someone had been killed in his care. It was something he did not take lightly.

"Do you want me to stick around for backup?" Mike asked more seriously.

"No." Jason could not afford to have someone else to look after.

"Alright. Be careful." Mike had been Jason's partner for three years and he knew better than to try to change his mind.

One footprint. Two hours of searching and that is all Jason had to show for it. There was no bullet case, no scuff mark from the kick of a gun, not even a gum wrapper. Other than one large footprint, the killer was clean. Jason was not sure if the footprint was linked, but he reported it and got a man called out to get an imprint just in case.

Jason did one more sweep of the area before calling it quits. He had the eerie feeling of being watched, but could not pinpoint the cause. Discouraged and exhausted, Jason returned to the station.

———

"Why don't you head home?" Graham asked, pouring himself a cup of coffee.

Jason did not hear him. He was sitting at the break room table staring into the black depth of a cup of coffee.

Graham tapped him lightly and Jason started, sloshing the coffee onto the table.

"Why don't you head home?" Graham repeated. "You're shot, Man. Give it some time to wear off."

"There was someone there." Jason ran his fingers into his hair.

"You're doing it again."

Jason stood and shoved his hands into his pockets. "Graham, I'm telling you, there was someone there. I could feel them watching me." His hand went toward his hair and he shoved it back into his pocket.

"What? You have some kind of super power sixth sense?" Graham joked weakly. "Listen, Jason, you've got to let it go. It wasn't your fault he got shot. He deserved it. You know, the whole 'God will give you what you dish out.'"

"That is what the world says, not what the Bible says," Jason answered distractedly.

"There's something about reaping what you sow in there," Graham countered. "I saw it on a church marquee."

"God is just, Graham, but God didn't shoot that robber tonight." Jason refused to be distracted. "Someone shot him. Right out of my hand. Whoever it is, he is still out there armed and dangerous."

"You think he was gunning for you?" Graham was serious.

"I don't think so. It was too planned out to be that far off. Whoever it was got in before the police line had been established, he was probably staked out to make sure the job got done right. Backup didn't arrive until after I was in the bank. He had to have been in place before that happened. The camera guy could have been a diversion…"

"Sounds logical so far," Graham observed.

"But why do it then?" Jason wondered aloud. "Unless it was to get my attention."

"You are afraid to go home." It was a statement, not an accusation.

For the first time Jason met Graham's eyes. "What if he is hurting me by hurting people around me? What if this was just a warning?"

"Hey, take it easy, Man. You are jumping to conclusions that don't exist and bending this thing way out of shape."

"Things have been so peaceful the last few years," Jason mumbled. "Why would it start now?"

"You must have had a rough childhood." Graham got a paper towel from beside the coffee maker and held it out to Jason. "You are starting to lose it, Jason. Clean up your mess and go home."

Jason dumped the untouched coffee down the drain.

"You're still sweating it," Graham observed. He was leaning against the door frame blowing gently across his steaming coffee.

"I can't shake it, Graham." Jason tossed the empty cup into the trash. "I didn't even hear anything. He just jerked and was gone."

"I don't want to sound cold, but this isn't the first stiff you've encountered on the job."

"I know."

"So why the big deal about this one?" Graham took a

sip before continuing. "Aren't you supposed to trust God and all that?"

Jason looked at him. "Seems kind of low to pull that card, don't you think?"

Graham shrugged.

"Just because I am a believer doesn't mean I'm perfect," Jason informed him with a twinge of irritation. "Yes, God is in control. But I am human. Sometimes it takes a man a little time to sort things out."

Graham looked thoughtful but did not reply.

Gathering his things Jason considered Graham's question as he wiped up the spilled coffee. It was true, but it was not what he wanted to hear.

"Lord, I can't have a theological discussion right now," Jason prayed silently. "I don't have the energy for it."

"I guess I'll head home," Jason mumbled to Graham. "Have a good night."

"It's two a.m." Graham was not going to drop it.

Ignoring the comment, Jason pushed the door open and trudged wearily out to his car.

Six

"Hello Seth."

"Hello Seth," Seth mocked irritably as he slouched in the stationary chair. "I'm sick of this."

Benjamin looked down at the young man. His bleach blond hair was uncombed and hung down over his ears. With his arms crossed defiantly, Seth was the perfect picture of a rebellious teen.

"So you got a gig planned for when you get out." Benjamin saw the answer in the boy's startled look.

"Nah, I'm going straight," Seth lied, checking Benjamin's face for belief.

"Uh huh."

"It's cool, Man," Seth went on. "I'm really catching all this look to the future stuff. I'm a new man."

Benjamin's gaze did not waver from Seth's eyes, and Seth shifted uncomfortably.

"Sorry Seth, you might be able to pull that over on a square. But not me. I haven't been square long enough to take that lame bait."

Seth frowned. "You don't believe me?" His innocent look had been perfected years ago.

"Get real, Seth. You've got you a gig lined up, and you're chafing to get at it."

Seth tried to object but Benjamin plowed on.

"You're not thinking future. Not long term. You're just

trying to get through this and on to your next hit. What is it? A robbery?"

Seth pouted.

"How old are you, Seth?" Benjamin demanded.

"Seventeen," Seth mumbled.

"And by the time you get out you will be almost…?" Benjamin pressed.

"Eighteen," Seth growled.

"You are turning eighteen two days after you get out. That means this is the last time you get a light slap on the hand. They will treat you like a real criminal once you turn eighteen, you dope." Benjamin caught himself. "Sorry, I shouldn't have called you a dope."

"I've been called worse." Seth was hard.

"Seth, don't you see? All this time I keep trying to tell you. There is a better way. You don't have to keep living like this."

Seth sat back with a dull look of boredom.

Benjamin shook his head and walked slowly to the far wall and back. "I don't even know why I care." Benjamin met Seth's questioning look. "Why should I care? It is your life. If you want to blow it and spend your life in the slammer with a bunch of sick jerks…" Benjamin looked away and let his breath out hard. "Why do I care?"

"Is this supposed to move me?" Seth was still glaring.

"No. No, sometimes I just wonder why God put me in this line of work." Benjamin sat down and folded his arms on the table. "So now what?"

Seth was not sure what Benjamin meant. He had the odd feeling that he should run, but repressed it and slouched further. This counselor was not like any he had ever had. "So you are a God guy." Seth said it accusingly. "And a square."

"Yes." There was no shame in his answer.

"You just came to push your religion on me." Before, this had always riled people who called themselves Christians, but the tall man was not bothered by the accusation.

"We've got thirty minutes," Benjamin told him with a quick glance at his watch. "Is that the topic you want to cover?"

"No."

"You are the one choosing." He was looking absently out the observation window behind Seth.

"You said you weren't always a square." Seth finally blurted. "What does that mean?"

"A square is someone who does things by the book. Someone who follows the rules and gets things honestly."

"I know what a square is," Seth said with disgust.

"So, I didn't always follow those rules." Benjamin adjusted the wedding ring on his finger. Seth had noticed it before, but the subject had not come up.

"You married?"

"Yep."

Seth felt like they had swapped roles. He was the one trying to pry answers out of the counselor. "Who to?" Seth asked.

Benjamin looked amused. "To my wife."

Seth rolled his eyes. "Duh."

"You asked." Benjamin grinned at him.

"I also asked about your pre-square days," Seth pointed out.

"I was in a gang of sorts. A little more complicated than that, but a gang is the easiest way to say it."

"A gangster?" Seth looked skeptical.

Benjamin laughed. "That was ten plus years ago, but I could do it again if I wanted."

Seth sat forward. "Yeah? You planning something?"

The amusement disappeared from Benjamin's face and Seth wished he had not asked.

"Do you realize what having a record does to your life?" Benjamin unfolded himself and towered over Seth. "While your friends are earning ten to twenty bucks an hour, you'll be trying to hang on with minimum wage. While they are dining out, you are splitting fifty cent soup mixes to try to make it to your next check. Seth, I've lived this, I know. Do you have any idea how hard it was for me to get where I am now?"

Seth didn't look up, but in his heart he knew this man was real.

"I applied to be on the police force, to be a fire fighter, even to work at a hospital. Each time it was the same. Once the record came up I was out the door." Without warning Benjamin squatted down so he was at Seth's eye level. "Seth, don't you understand? This is what I'm trying to save you from."

———

"You here again?"

Jason grinned sheepishly at Mike. "You too huh?"

Mike scanned the area. "I can't make sense of it, Jason. Something big happened here last night."

"Have they identified the robber?"

"Yeah, but from what I heard he doesn't have a serious record. He's some petty first timer. His name was…" Mike thought for a moment. "Ethen Puller? I think that's right. The record department is still working on the full report, what I got was just word of mouth. Seems like this Ethen Puller dropped out of the sky, and decided to rob a bank. The chief ordered a broader search to be made to see if we can get anything else on him."

"It doesn't match up." Jason muttered.

They poked around the crime scene, doing their best to stay out of the way of the investigators. The sun had been up for hours, but it did little to penetrate the crisp fall morning.

"Did you go home last night?" Mike opened a fresh water bottle and took a swig.

"No. Ellen wasn't expecting me so I just drove around."

"And came here." Mike laughed. "Even before you made that face, I knew you did."

"Okay, so I did." Jason took the water bottle Mike offered and broke the seal. "I just looked around."

"On the roof?" Mike pressed.

Jason glanced at him over his water.

"Did you find anything?"

Jason recapped the bottle and sighed. "Nothing. Not even a scrap of a clue."

"Hmm."

"The angle of the entry point would have put the gun man up there." Jason pointed to the one story office building across the street. "He would have had a clear shot from there."

Mike observed the setting thoughtfully "Know anyone who could have done it?"

"I know a few," Jason admitted. "But there's no motive. Why kill him after he was arrested?"

"Maybe he knew something," Mike offered.

"No, he would have tried to talk to me inside if he knew his life was in danger." Jason frowned. Maybe Ethen had not known the sniper was waiting.

"You got something?" Mike asked seeing his frown.

"No." Jason's fingers combed through his dark hair. "What about you? You have any clues?"

Mike finished off his water before answering. "There are a couple of guys, but like you, I don't see a motive."

"Seems we have a motley group of friends," Jason observed dryly.

Mike laughed. "Hey, it pays to keep things well rounded."

"You two still hanging around here?"

They looked up to see the police chief striding toward them.

"Sure, Chief. We want to get the dirt on this while it is fresh." Mike's grin was contagious.

"If you two weren't my best team I'd throw you out for snooping," Chief Pawlson quipped.

"If you weren't the best chief, we'd quit," Jason shot back.

Pawlson laughed. "Alright, flattering aside, boys. I've got a good old fashioned mystery on my hands, and not a clue in a twenty mile radius. You were here last night, do you have any leads?"

"Sorry Chief, we are as lost as you on this one. Jason here has been giving it a double shift."

"I thought I gave you the day off."

"He didn't take it." Mike cut in before Jason could answer. "He's a regular Sherlock Holmes. Ain't that right, Laddie?"

Jason shot him a friendly glare. "Lay off, Watson."

"Let's get serious, boys. This is not a joking matter," Pawlson said gruffly putting a stop to the playful banter.

They sobered up instantly. "I know Chief. Maybe we need a little space from it," Mike told him. "We've been pulling double shifts all week."

"I know. I was going to give you both some vacation time before all this broke out." His gesture enveloped the entire area. The crime tape fluttered like streamers in the wind. Uniformed officers were spread out casing the grounds for any scrap of evidence. Other than the type of bullet Ethen Puller was killed with, they had nothing to go on.

Jason and Mike felt the urgency of the hunt. "Is there anything else we can do?"

"No, not now." Pawlson removed his hat and wiped his brow. "Go home and get some rest. I have a feeling I am going to need you later. Oh, and Jason."

"Yes, Sir?"

"Call that boy's caseworker. He's getting to be a regular at the office and Nancy wants him off her hands."

"Yes, Sir." Jason groaned inwardly. A talk with a nosy caseworker was the last thing he needed right now.

"Call us the minute you find something." Mike stepped aside to allow another officer access to the chief.

"Will do," Pawlson answered absently as he scanned a report he had just been handed.

Mike slapped Jason on the shoulder as they headed back to the cruiser. "Well ol' boy, let's get some shut eye."

"Sure."

SEVEN

"Daddy's home!" Benjamin fairly ran into Jason's legs as he entered the house.

Jason ruffled his hair. "Hey Benji boy. Did you take good care of Mommy for me?"

The little boy stood on Jason's shoes and clung to his legs. His little voice rose and fell as he recounted the events of his day. Jason caught a word here and there as he greeted Ellen and stowed his bag. He picked up Benjamin and kissed his head. "You did good, little man."

"You look tired." Ellen observed setting the salad bowl on the table.

"I am. Did you hear about the bank case on the news?"

"Yesterday?" Ellen got the dressing from the refrigerator. "Was he the one who was mysteriously killed?"

"Yeah, he was shot right out of my hand." Jason got the silverware from the drawer as he spoke.

She put her hand on his shoulder. "I'm so sorry, Jason."

"Just a little jerk. I didn't hear or see anything."

"Honey," She waited until he met her eyes, "we are not having soup."

Jason looked at the handful of spoons he was holding. "Aren't we having ice cream?"

Ellen laughed. "I guess we could."

"Good, I'll put spoons on so we don't have to get them later." Jason put the extras back into their place and added some forks to his stash. "Sorry, Ellen. I just keep mulling it over, but there isn't any conclusion. I can't figure out why it happened. Then there is that crazy kid's caseworker who keeps hanging around for an interview."

The timer interrupted him and they dropped the subject. Ellen got the casserole from the oven and put it on the table.

"Time to eat." She called loudly. Benj appeared in the doorway and scrambled into his seat. Kara came a moment later lugging Levi in her arms. Jason put him in the highchair and they sat down to eat.

Benj bowed his head and folded his hands expectantly.

"Benj, would you like to pray for us tonight?" Jason asked.

"Yep." Benj closed his eyes tightly. "God, thank you for all this yummy food and for daddy coming home an not being hurt or dead…"

Jason glanced at Ellen and saw she was smiling slightly.

"What do you tell him when I'm gone?" Jason asked when Benj was done praying.

"We pray for you," Ellen answered simply.

"Well I appreciate it, but…I don't know if it is good for him to always think I'm dead."

"We pray for Mr. Mike too," Benj added proudly.

"Good. I don't know what I would do without him." Jason pushed his food around on the plate.

Ellen put her hand on Jason's arm. "Maybe we should save the ice cream for another night."

"You guys can still have it." Jason pushed back from the table. "I think I'll go lay down for a while if that's okay."

"I think it is a good idea. You'll feel better once you get some rest. Do you want to call the caseworker so you can get that off your mind?"

"No, I'll call him later. He probably just wants to split hairs over what happened."

Ellen smiled. "Go take a nap. You are a regular grouch."

Jason laughed and kissed her lightly. "Goodnight all." He said grandly before exiting.

————

"Hello Nancy."

"He's not in." Nancy's answer was blunt.

Benjamin went to the counter and leaned in confidentially. "Does Roper really work here?"

She looked annoyed. "Listen, Buddy."

"Hey, don't get riled." Benjamin put up his palms and backed away. "I can take a hint. You have my number. Let him know I stopped by."

"For the hundredth time," Nancy muttered.

Benjamin laughed and left the office. An officer was walking toward the door as Benjamin came out. "Hey, do you have a second?" Benjamin asked.

Graham stopped and waited.

"Do you know Roper?"

"Roper who?" Graham wondered where this guy had come from.

"Jason Roper. I hear he works here but I can't seem to get in touch with him."

Graham was skeptical.

"I'm the caseworker for Seth Blandy."

"Ah!" Graham laughed. "Sorry, we get some weird people who hang around here."

"I'm not promising to be normal," Benjamin replied. "But seriously, I would like to discuss Seth's case with the officer involved."

"Did you let Nancy know?"

Benjamin could tell by the slight upward curve of the officer's mouth, that this had become some kind of inside joke.

"Yes."

"Well, she will let him know." Graham might as well

have said 'the end'.

"Right. Thanks." Benjamin went to his car and got in. He had been trying to get in touch with Roper for several weeks. Obviously dear Nancy was not passing on the same message he was leaving.

Benjamin backed out and drove aimlessly down the road. The sun had slid down toward the horizon by the time Benjamin made it back to the hotel. Out of habit he checked the lot before parking. A junker parked at the end of the lot caught his eye. Benjamin pulled in leaving an open parking space on the driver's side. He retrieved his Glock from the glove box, slid it into its holster and shoved that under his belt clipping it expertly into place.

"Okay, Lord. Here it goes," Benjamin said aloud. He grabbed his briefcase, pocketed his car keys and took out his room card. "Help me to be wise." Taking a deep breath he let it out slowly and got out. Moving confidently, Benjamin entered the hotel lobby. He took the elevator to the second floor, if he had to face them he wanted to avoid doing it on the stairs. There was no one in the hall. He went to his room, slid the key and stepped to the side as he pushed the door open. Nothing. Benjamin hesitated, something was not right. Releasing the door, he let it slam shut. Going back to the elevator, he pressed the button a couple of times as if that would speed it up. The tense feeling was growing stronger. Benjamin pushed the button again. The elevator opened and the man inside stepped over to let Benjamin in. He was in his late forties, a sport jacket and dress pants gave him a wealthy air. Benjamin's eyes dropped to the gun the man held.

"Get in."

For an instant Benjamin weighed his options. They weren't good.

"Get in," The man ordered, keeping his voice low.

Benjamin did as he was told, standing uncomfortably

close to the barrel of the gun. The doors shut behind him and they started moving up.

"I didn't want to go up," Benjamin informed him.

"Well, you aren't calling the shots."

As he had hoped, the man jabbed the gun at Benjamin to add authority to his words.

Using his right hand Benjamin slammed the gun into the elevator wall and threw his right shoulder against the man. The sound of the report was deafening in the tight quarters. Still gripping the man's gun hand Benjamin jerked him forward. The gun went off again and the bullet imbedded into the silver plated panel. The man was off balance and Benjamin used his momentum to twist the gun from his grasp. Shoving him to the floor Benjamin stood over him. "I don't want to go up." Benjamin said through clenched teeth. He hit the ground floor button and waited as they approached the 9th floor. Benjamin pulled back the slide, there was a bullet in the chamber. He ejected the clip, two more bullets there. The man shifted and Benjamin clicked the clip back in place.

"I would be really still if I were you," Benjamin observed, he could tell the man was calculating something. "If you think a strong kick will bring me down, you are wrong." Benjamin heard the elevator ding. "I'll put a bullet in you before I fall." Benjamin promised as the doors slid open.

A wide eyed cleaning lady stood in front of a muscular man who looked as if he had grown up in a gym.

"Drop it." Benjamin demanded before the doors were fully open. When the man hesitated Benjamin let a bullet whistle by the gym model's ear. "I said drop it."

He obeyed sullenly and the bulky handgun clattered to the floor.

Benjamin moved forward to keep the doors from closing. "Get in."

The man on the elevator floor kicked Benjamin's leg hard, but Benjamin had been expecting it. Rotating slightly, he stomped on the man's foot causing him to cry out. "That was a warning," Benjamin told him without taking his eyes from the man standing before him. "I said get in."

They moved forward, but Benjamin gestured with his gun at the man. "Not you. I'll take the lady, you take the stairs. Miss, pick up his gun and get in here."

She whimpered some Spanish and retrieved the gun. Keeping his weapon trained on the big guy, Benjamin took the gun from her.

Still whimpering she stepped over the prone man's legs and took her place in the elevator. Benjamin moved back into the elevator and its doors slid closed.

"Sorry about all this," Benjamin told her shoving the gun he had been using into his belt. He covered his remaining captive with the bulky weapon the cleaning lady had retrieved. "I'm going to call the police." He informed her gently, pulling his cell phone from his pocket.

"You let him get away. He was a very bad man," she said in a burst of passion.

"I didn't want both of them in here with me." Benjamin held the phone to his ear. "I can take care of this bimbo here, but I'd rather not mess with that buff dude up there." He turned his attention to the phone. "Yes, I would like to report an attempted kidnapping."

EIGHT

"This is Jason." Jason was still groggy from sleep.

"Hey, Man. Did you catch the latest?"

"This is my night off, Mike," Jason reminded him. "Unlike you I don't spend it hugging my radio."

"Aw, come on, Jason," Mike said eagerly. "This is big."

"Tell me what happened." Jason threw back the covers and sat up, rubbing his face to wake himself.

"There was an attempted kidnapping at the Royal Hotel down on 108th. The guy they tried to knap turned out to be some kind of karate expert or something. He took their guns and both men were captured...."

"Is that Mike?"

Jason looked up to see Ellen silhouetted in the doorway. She put her fists on her hips. He nodded and attempted to smooth his hair.

"Tell him you have the night off." She did not even try to whisper.

"Honey, he's excited about a kidnapping on the edge of town. The guy got away or something." Jason held the phone a little further from his ear for a moment. "Excuse me," he droned dully. "He didn't get away, he blew the socks off the crooks. Quote, unquote."

"You are not taking me seriously," Mike complained.

"Mike, Ellen is telling me to hang up," Jason informed him. "I kind of missed part of what you said." Jason put the phone on speaker so Ellen could listen.

"This is big stuff. This guy knew what he was doing. He told Graham he knew something was up before he parked his car. Do you think he is looking for a job?"

"He probably already has one," Ellen commented.

"Fine, miss the biggest event in the history of this force. It's no skin off my teeth."

Jason laughed. "That is a disgusting saying."

"Jason Roper, I don't know why I even bother."

Even over the phone, Jason could tell Mike was grinning.

"Okay, okay. What's his name and I'll look him up."

"Benjamin…something. Burr maybe? Something like that. He didn't want his full name on the record but I think Graham has it." Mike paused. "You still there?"

"Yeah." Jason called over his shoulder as he headed for the bathroom.

"He's getting dressed," Ellen informed Mike.

"Hot dog!" Mike cleared his throat. "Sorry. Um… have a nice evening."

"You can't come." Jason immerged from the bathroom wearing black cargo pants and a dark jacket he was zipping up.

"Why not?" Mike demanded.

"Remember when we were talking about the guys we knew?" Jason did not wait for an answer. "Benjamin Curr is one of mine. Good bye, Mike." Jason ended the call and slid the phone into his pocket

"I thought you were going to take the night off and get some rest," Ellen pointed out.

"Ellen, I haven't seen Benjamin in over five years. This is Benjamin we are talking about. The guy who saved my life, the guy our kid's named after. He's the best friend I've had besides you."

Ellen laughed. "I guess you had better hurry."

"Thanks, El." Jason meant it. "I'll bring him back with

me if I can."

———

"Hey Graham, you guys have this place cleaned up nicely," Jason observed looking around.

"Mike told me you were coming out."

"Here I am. What else did he tell you?"

"He said you wanted a word with the hero guy."

Jason grinned. "I cannot tell a lie."

"I don't see why you will drive all the way across town to see him, but you won't return his calls." Graham waved to the other cruiser that was pulling past. "See you later, James. Have a good night."

"What did you mean by that?" Jason asked following Graham to the last police car.

Graham shrugged. "Benjamin is the case worker for the Blandy kid."

"Nancy never gave me his name," Jason mumbled.

Graham got into the cruiser. "Let that be a lesson to you," he chided playfully.

"Get out of here." Jason pushed the door shut. "Hey wait."

Graham rolled the window down. "Yeah?"

"What room is he in?"

"He was in 207, but I'm pretty sure he will be moving to another room after all this."

"Thanks, Graham. Have a good night."

Jason was stopped at the front desk by a thick security guard who insisted on calling up to Benjamin's room. He then escorted Jason to room 207.

The door opened and there was Benjamin, just like he had been ten years ago.

"It's good to see you, Benjamin." Jason held out his hand a bit awkwardly. Benjamin took it and pulled him into a hug.

"You too, Man. It's been a while. Come on in if you

dare." Benjamin stepped out of the way so Jason could enter. "Thanks Joe, I think he will behave."

The security guard did not seem to catch the joke, but he left them alone.

"I'd be scared to get on that guy's bad side." Jason looked around the little room. There was stuff scattered around, but apparently Benjamin did not have much to scatter.

"You are limping," Jason observed.

"The old arthritis is bothering me again," Benjamin answered in a creaky old voice.

"You have arthritis?"

Benjamin laughed at Jason's surprised expression. "No, the guy in the elevator kicked me."

"What guy?"

"The one trying to kidnap me. I was expecting the kick, but he hit a lot harder than I thought he would. I guess he caught my ankle just right."

"Is there anything I can do?"

Benjamin shrugged. "I'll get it checked out tomorrow sometime. So, enough about me, how have you been?" Benjamin gestured to the only chair and sat on the dresser.

Jason took the seat. "Busy. Really busy."

"Yeah?"

"Police work is draining me. I keep getting hit with these odd ball cases, and right when I've almost got one sorted out, the next one hits."

Benjamin could see the effects of the strain in Roper's features. He looked worn and tired.

"Like a kid shooting you in the face?"

"Yeah, sorry about not calling you back. Nancy never gave me a name, and as a rule I don't like case workers." Jason looked up at him. "Are you really a case worker now?"

Benjamin made a face. "Not exactly. More of a special ops counselor guy. They called me in for this case. They thought

I could make some headway."

"Have you?" Jason asked.

"Well, Roper, do you go by Roper, or Jason?"

Jason shrugged. "Either is fine. I answer to both."

Benjamin noticed the ring on Jason's finger. "Hey, hey! The bachelor has settled down."

Jason nodded and held up the ring proudly. "I told Ellen I'd bring you to meet her. I was thinking that maybe you would sleep better if you had a different bed."

"You mean a different location?" Benjamin glanced around the messy room. "Sure, but I don't mind one more night here."

"If you don't mind a little extra noise we'd love to have you stay with us."

"I don't think so." Benjamin was serious.

Jason frowned a little. "Okay."

"Not that I don't like you, Roper. I appreciate what you are trying to do, but if there are thugs after me, I don't want to bring your family into this. At least not until I know why they were here."

"I understand." Jason let the subject drop, grateful for such a good friend. "How's your family?"

"Wonderful." Benjamin pulled out his wallet and fished for a picture. "There you go." He handed it across to Jason. "That little pot belly my wife has is number five."

"Boy or girl?" Jason asked looking over the little group. He could tell they were a lively bunch by the way they were grinning at the camera.

"Girl," Benjamin answered sliding off the dresser to look with Jason. "We don't have a name picked out yet because she's still pretty new."

Jason laughed. "I understand. We didn't name Levi until after he was born."

"Do you have a picture?" Benjamin asked.

Jason handed the picture back. "I don't carry one."

"Probably wise. I don't see much action these days." Benjamin put the photo away and picked up a shirt from the floor. "At least not until I got here."

"So tell me about this Blandy kid." Jason retrieved a couple of papers from the worn carpet and stacked them neatly on the table.

"Seth? Well, he had me worried at first. It wasn't that he claimed to have shot you. Which, by the way, is not nice to do to people."

"Hey, I didn't ask him to shoot me."

"Anyway, it isn't that he knows he shot you, it is deeper. When I first met him, he would easily have done it again." Benjamin was folding the clothes as Jason tossed them onto the bed. "I really hit him hard with it last time I was there. Not literally," Benjamin clarified. "Those guys are treated like babies by their family, and they just assume the rest of the world will do the same. I am pretty sure he's already got a gig planned for when he gets out. What do you do with someone like that?"

Jason shrugged. "I guess pray for them and keep hitting them with the truth."

"I just about lost it last time I was there. He's so stupid. There's no concept of where this will lead in five years, or even one year." Benjamin looked up from the clothes. "Don't tell anyone I said that."

"Sure." Jason stopped cleaning and looked around.

"You alright?" Benjamin asked.

"Are there spiders in here?" Jason asked feeling under the decorative edge of the dresser.

Benjamin smiled at their old code word. "Beats me." Benjamin joined Jason in scouring the room. They were not looking for insects, they were looking for bugs.

"Maybe you should get a new room." Jason pointed out when they found what they were looking for.

Benjamin nodded "Yeah, I think I will."

NINE

Seth sat with his head resting on his fists and his elbows on the table.

"Sorry I'm late, Seth." Benjamin limped across the room to his chair.

"What happened to you, twist your ankle?"

"Not exactly. I'll get it checked once we are done here."

"You think it's broken?"

Benjamin shrugged. "Could be fractured, but I don't think it is broken."

"What happened?" Seth leaned over to look under the table. He could not see anything except Benjamin's pant leg.

Benjamin did not answer right away. "Seth, what are you going to do when you get out?"

Seth was not expecting the question. He blinked dumbly at Benjamin.

"I'm really not sure what to do with you. Your case worker called me in to help you, but I don't think I'm doing you any good. I come in here and blab for half an hour, then we part ways and you dump what I said right outside the door."

"I think about it," Seth told him. "Some of it."

Benjamin slapped two pictures on the table. "You ever see these guys before?"

Seth glanced at them. "No."

"You sure?"

"Yeah, I'm sure."

"That's interesting, especially since this man visited you last week. The guard identified him this morning."

Seth squirmed in his seat.

"What did you tell him?'

"Nothing."

"Just like you never saw him?" Benjamin slid the picture closer. His voice dropped low and hard. "You told him I was in a gang. You told him I could run my own if I wanted."

Seth got up and backed away from the table. "Let me out," he called banging on the locked door. There was no response from the outside.

Benjamin pushed himself up from the table and pocketed the pictures.

Cold fear crept up Seth's spine. "I didn't tell him anything," he lied miserably.

"Don't lie to me, Seth." Benjamin's voice did not change as Seth cringed against the door.

"He asked," Seth finally blurted. "I only told him because he asked."

Benjamin looked at him coolly. "Sit down."

Seth hesitated, then meekly obeyed.

Benjamin shook his head and Seth looked around in time to see someone disappear from the viewing window.

Seth jumped to his feet, thought better of it, and sank back down into the chair. It was no longer difficult to picture Benjamin as the leader of a gang.

"Why did he want to know about me?" Benjamin pressed.

"I don't know," Seth muttered. "He said something about you being useful. Said he would give me a share once I got out."

"Mr. Lest is in custody."

"You are lying." Seth dared to meet his steady gaze.

"I got the mug shot from the cops this morning." Benjamin limped back to his seat. "Do you realize what your little stunt did? Or did you forget to think farther out?"

Seth dropped his eyes and did not answer.

"I'll tell you. You squealed to Mr. Lest and he picked up a hulk and some other dude someplace and camped out at the hotel. At gunpoint – which means someone could have been killed – they held Mrs. Mendez, the cleaning lady, and scared her so bad that she quit her job. She has four kids to feed at home, but she's too scared to go back. They kidnapped someone, and who knows what else they would have done if the police hadn't showed up."

"I didn't do it."

"Not directly, but you had a hand in it."

"I don't see how," Seth grumbled. "What does that have to do with me telling them about you?"

"I will try to spell this out more clearly. I was staying at the hotel. I was the one they tried to kidnap. I could have been killed. She could have been killed." Benjamin nodded at the window and Seth heard the click of the lock. "Think about it Seth. One choice has a ripple effect on yourself and others. You are not the focal point, but what you do makes a difference."

Seth saw him wince as he got to his feet. His limp was worse and Seth could tell he was trying hard to control it.

"I'm sorry you got hurt."

Benjamin smiled. "Thanks." It was the first sign of hope he had seen in Seth.

———

"Relax, Jason." Ellen put her hand on Jason's and he started. "What?"

"I said relax." Ellen pointed to the playground. "Why don't you go play with the kids? They need their Daddy."

"You're right, El. I'm sorry." Jason got up off the hard picnic table bench and stretched.

"I know a lot has happened this week."

"That's no excuse, Ellen. I've been constantly pouring over this case and I need to put work aside."

She smiled. "It would be nice."

Jason nodded. "Thanks for saying it."

Still smiling, Ellen gave him a gentle push toward the play equipment. "Go give those babies of yours something to squeal about."

"Daddy's coming!" Kara yelled excitedly. "Run!"

Jason jogged the short distance to the playground and joined in the jolly free for all.

Ellen smiled. This was good for Jason.

She noticed he paused for a moment, his gaze diverted from the giggling children. She followed it to a tall man who was making his way along the sidewalk. He wore a boot on his left leg and limped on it as he walked.

"You can't get me, Daddy!" Kara called from the top of the slide.

The man glanced up with a smile. It faded a little and he looked forward again as if he had not seen Jason. Ellen turned her attention back to Jason. His attention was diverted as well, willfully so. He looked thoughtful and shot one more quick glance toward the man before ducking under the play equipment after Benj.

Ellen knew they had seen each other. She got up and strolled casually to the playground.

"Who was that?" she asked as Jason made a half-hearted grab at Kara's ankle.

Jason did not look back. "Benjamin."

"You didn't even say 'hi' to him," Ellen observed.

"He's in hot water right now and wants to protect you and the kids."

"What kind of hot water?"

"That's the problem," Jason answered seriously. "He doesn't know."

T<small>EN</small>

"Hi Mike," Jason hailed him as he got out of his civilian car.
"Hey."

"How was your day off?" Jason asked with a twinkle in his eye. "Were you able to tear yourself from the radio?"

"Hey, that was hot stuff on Thursday." Mike pretended to be annoyed. "You gotta admit it was pretty impressive."

"I didn't get all the details." Jason held the door open and waited for Mike.

"You should get them. The guy wrestled this other guy down in the elevator, and took his gun right out of his hand. That is what he used to save the cleaning lady."

"He wasn't armed before?" Jason asked knowing the answer.

"How should I know? You wouldn't let me near him."

Jason laughed. "Well some friends I'd rather keep to myself."

Mike went inside and Jason followed him.

"Hey James, any leads on the sniper?"

James finished his sip of coffee before responding. "Nope. Criminal has something on the robber though. Swing by the office and Clem will fill you in."

"Thanks."

They stopped in and Clem filled them in on what they had on the murdered man. Ethen Puller had a couple of petty thefts under his belt but nothing worth talking about.

It seemed the bank robbery was his biggest job. As for the sniper there were still no leads. Clem complained about the lack of evidence and the lack of motive. They thanked him and went to pick up their patrol route from Nancy.

"Glad you came in boys," She said by way of greeting. "Graham was wondering if you two would have a minute to question the man involved in the hotel kidnapping. He's due in…" She glanced at the little clock on her screen. "about ten minutes to make a statement."

Mike noticed Jason stiffen, but said nothing.

Nancy looked over her glasses. "And Jason," she waited until he looked up, "call that case worker."

"I got it covered, Nancy," Jason assured her.

"You okay with questioning him?" Mike asked as they made their way back to the recording room.

"Yeah."

Mike was not convinced. "You sure? I could do it alone if you need me to."

One side of Jason's mouth went up and he glanced over at the man beside him. "As long as it doesn't get around that Benjamin and I are friends, I think it will be fine."

"Alright, you've never seen him before."

Jason rolled his eyes. "Just don't overdo it."

———

"The world is overrun with crooks and stupid people."

Ellen, Kara, and Benj looked up from the book they were reading.

"That's a cheery greeting," Ellen observed.

"It is not a greeting, it is a fact," Jason informed her, stowing his bag in the coat closet.

"Well, then." Ellen patted the couch beside her. "Just sit yourself down here beside the only normal people in the world."

Kara giggled and Benj clambered onto Jason's lap.

"What great work are we reading?" Jason asked peering over Benj's head.

"Corduroy." Ellen informed him seriously.

"Ah. That one has a nice police man and a hug in it." Jason leaned his head against the wall and stretched out his long legs.

Benj twisted around to look up at Jason. "Daddy, did you irrigate someone today?"

Jason lifted his head and looked down at his son. He glanced at Ellen and whispered, "Is he asking if I shot someone?"

Ellen started laughing. She attempted to answer but could not and shook her head instead.

Benj looked happily from one to the other. "Well?" he finally asked. "Did you?"

"What do you mean, Benj?" Jason asked, trying hard to look serious. With Ellen shaking with suppressed laughter beside him, it was impossible to keep from smiling.

"Ask them a bunch of questions," Kara answered for him.

"Oh," Jason bit his lip to keep from laughing. "I did interrogate someone today."

"A crook?" Kara asked with interest.

"No, a good guy."

"A stupid people?" Benj asked.

Ellen grinned at Jason with a "you said it" look.

Levi hollered from the bedroom and Ellen went to get him.

"No, a good guy. He was making a statement. That means he was telling what happened."

"What happened?" Kara asked.

"Well, a bad man had a gun and this good guy took it from him."

"Did the bad guy get away?" Benj was wide eyed.

"No. Graham and James and a couple of other officers caught the bad guys and put them in jail."

"Oh." Benj and Kara said together. In their minds all was well.

There was a knock at the door.

"Wonder who that is?" Ellen emerged from the hallway with Levi on her hip. "You stay put. I'll get it."

She went to the door and opened it. A little startled cry escaped her as Mike barged in supporting the man she had seen earlier that evening at the park. He was deathly pale and would have crumpled to the floor if Mike had not been beside him. His face was dirty and Ellen could not tell the dirt from the bruises.

"Get down." Jason was across the room in an instant. Kara and Benj dropped expertly to the floor as Jason swung the door shut and locked it behind them in one quick motion. "I'm really sorry, Roper." Benjamin's voice was weak. "I didn't know." He leaned heavily against the wall. Jason and Mike helped him across the room and into the kitchen. Ellen pulled a chair out for him, but they lowered him to the floor instead.

"He'll be safer down here, Ellen. He's not real steady," Mike told her.

"I wouldn't have come…" Benjamin looked up at Ellen who, still in shock, was covering her mouth with her hand.

She dropped her hand, trying to look as if this was an everyday occurrence. "We are glad you came. We want to help you."

"Keep them covered," Jason told Mike. He did a quick check of the house to make sure the rest of the doors and windows were secure.

"What happened?" Jason asked when he returned, glancing around to make sure his family was safe.

Benjamin lay with his eyes closed, his breathing controlled.

"I found him stumbling along the road," Mike told them. "Kind of hunched over like he was trying to keep out of sight."

"Daddy?" Kara, who was clinging to Ellen's leg sounded scared.

"It's alright, Kara." Ellen petted Kara's dark wavy hair.

Benj approached cautiously, watching with interest as Jason covered Benjamin with a warm blanket he had brought from the bedroom.

"Benjamin, can you hear me?" Jason was gingerly feeling his limbs. "Do you hurt anywhere?"

The slightest smile curved Benjamin's tight lips, his controlled breathing continued.

"I would translate that as 'everywhere,'" Mike answered for him.

"Where's his shoe?" Kara asked.

Jason pulled back the blanket. Benjamin's left sock was caked with dirt.

"You're very attentive, Kara." Jason pulled the blanket back over Benjamin's swollen foot.

She smiled shyly at her father's praise.

Setting Levi on the counter, Ellen got a glass of water. "Here, Jason. Give him this."

Jason propped him up and Mike put the glass to his mouth. Benjamin managed a tiny sip before turning his head away.

"Someone roughed him up pretty bad." Mike pointed out the black ring that was forming around Benjamin's eye.

"Do you think we should take him to the emergency room?" Ellen asked moving the active Levi to her other hip. He wanted very much to get down and howled to show his displeasure.

Benjamin stirred at the sound. "Roper, I'm sorry." The words were barely audible.

"Relax, Benjamin. You did the right thing."

"He doesn't want to go to the hospital," Mike informed them. "I tried that first. He was pretty adamant." Mike looked at Benjamin's prone form. "He was a bit more lively when I picked him up. I didn't know where else to take him."

"We can't just leave him on the kitchen floor," Ellen protested. "What if he has internal injuries?"

"What do you think, Mike?" Jason asked.

"I don't know." Mike sat back on his heels. "I guess you've got to keep him."

ELEVEN

"How do you feel?" Ellen asked setting the fresh glass of water on the nightstand.

Kara bent a straw and stuck it into the glass, keeping a wary eye on Benjamin.

Benjamin's good eye blinked up at them, the other was almost swollen shut. He groaned softly.

"Just rest. We didn't mean to disturb you." Ellen ushered Kara out of the room. A few minutes later the door opened again. Benjamin turned his head slightly to see who it was.

A little boy looked back at him over the edge of the bed.

"You have a black eye," Benj observed.

Benjamin did his best to smile. "Who are you?" his voice sounded choked and raspy.

"Benj. But that is just my short name. My long name is the same as yours and I can write it out myself."

"How old are you, Benj?" Benjamin asked.

"Five."

"I've got a little boy who is five." Benjamin coughed and groaned.

"Mr. Mike said somebody roughed you up." Benj peered over the bed. "I asked Daddy what that means before he went to work. It means they hit you a lot."

"Is your daddy gone?"

"Yep. He was on duty today."

"He's a good man," Benjamin sighed.

"Benjamin Titus Roper you get out of here," Ellen scolded in a low tone. She steered him out of the room with a hand on his back. "Mr. Benjamin is trying to rest." She turned back to Benjamin. "I'm very sorry."

"Does Roper come back for lunch or something?" Benjamin asked hoarsely.

Ellen looked at the wall clock. "He'll be back in about an hour if nothing comes up."

"I need to talk to him," Benjamin told her. "Will you tell him?"

"Yes. Get some rest. I'll send him in when he comes."

———

"Mike, did you hear? They found the sniper's gun." Graham burst into the break room. "Where's Jason?"

"He's on highway patrol." Mike, seated at the table, pushed out the chair across from him with his foot. "Where did they find it?"

Graham ignored the chair. "It was stashed a couple of blocks from the bank. Someone tipped us off to a drug deal and the gun came up in the raid. The marks on the bullet match the barrel to a T."

"Any idea who it belongs to?"

"No. Not yet. Forensics is tracing it, but it has apparently changed hands a number of times in the last year or so."

"Hey, a lead is a lead. Jason will be glad to hear it."

"How did the statement for the hotel case go? I sure appreciate you guys taking it. I was dealing with a domestic case. You know how messy those can get."

"Tell me about it," Mike agreed. "The statement went pretty well, the odd thing is I picked up the guy last night and he had been roughed up pretty bad."

"Did you find out who did it?"

"No. He was too out of it to be of any help. I've got James

staked out to watch the house."

"What house?" Graham demanded. "You took him home?"

"Not quite." Mike remembered Jason's request for secrecy. "I was closer to Jason's when I picked him up."

"So he's at Jason's? Why didn't you take him to the hospital?"

"Some people prefer to avoid that joint."

Graham understood. "Does the chief know?"

"I put a report on his desk."

Graham grinned.

"I thought I'd cover my back. Maybe I forgot where the reports go."

"Maybe. You have had a lot on your mind." Graham poured himself some coffee and leaned his back against the counter. "Now that we've moved forward on the sniper case we get a new complication on the hotel deal."

An all vehicles report came over the radio and Graham dumped his coffee into the sink. "That's us."

———

Benjamin heard the phone and attempted to sit up. Everything hurt so evenly that it was hard to pinpoint just one part.

The door opened, Benjamin looked over at the little darkeyed girl who stood in the doorway.

"Could you get that phone?" Benjamin asked weakly.

"I'm not supposed to come in here," Kara answered in a soft voice.

"I think it is important."

She disappeared for a moment and Benjamin heard her shouted request for permission. She reappeared and got the phone from the dresser and walked it over to him.

Benjamin worked his arm out from under the covers, he felt as if it were encased in iron. He took the phone and hit redial. He paused to look at his hand. His little finger was splinted.

"How old are you?" Benjamin was not sure what she was waiting for.

"Seven." Kara stared at him with interest.

"That's a good age." Benjamin closed his eyes and laid the phone beside his head. He would ask about the splint later.

"Hello? Is anyone there?" A lady's voice came over the line.

"I'm sorry, who is this?" He had missed the introduction.

"Your number registers as Seth's counselor. Is that who you are?" She was obviously new.

"You shouldn't tell me who I am. What if I had stolen this phone?" Benjamin informed her adjusting the phone so he could hear better.

She hesitated. "Your voice sounds different."

"I am Seth's counselor," Benjamin assured her. "I'm guessing you were calling because I am late."

"Well, yes." She was now being overly cautious.

"Something unexpected came up. I'm not going to make it today. Could you tell Seth that I am sorry, and that I'll try to make it next week?"

"You are scheduled to meet with him Monday."

"Yes. But I won't be able to make it until at least next Thursday. It will give him some time to read the book I gave him."

"I'll pass on your message."

Benjamin could tell by the distracted way she said it, that she was still taking down his message. "Thank you." He hung up and looked over at Kara who, having gained entrance, seemed in no hurry to leave.

"So you are seven?" Benjamin observed. "That makes you the oldest right?"

"Yes. My name is Kara." Her smile was identical to Roper's.

"I see. Kara, do you know who put this splint on my hand?" He held it up with some difficulty so she could see.

"The doctor did," she answered simply.

"What doctor?"

Kara looked thoughtful. "I don't remember his name."

"Did your Dad take me to the hospital?"

"Daddy said he wanted to explain that to you. We aren't supposed to."

"So he did," Benjamin muttered. That would mean there would be a record, a paper trail that would lead them here. He looked over at the window.

"You can't escape because Daddy says you are too beat up." Benj had joined his sister at the bedside.

"Who said I was escaping?" Benjamin asked. He was annoyed to have been read so easily.

"That's what Daddy said," Benj replied.

Benjamin made a face. "Thanks, Roper."

"Why do you call Daddy Roper?" Kara asked.

"I knew your Daddy a long time ago," Benjamin explained vaguely.

There was some noise from the front of the house and Jason 'helloed' his family.

"Daddy's home!"

They jostled each other in their haste to get out of the room, and Benjamin was left alone. He waited, knowing Roper would come.

A few minutes later Jason appeared in the doorway. "Well, you look…"

"Let's not talk about how I look," Benjamin interrupted. "I think I'll feel better if you didn't."

"How do you feel?" Jason pushed the door closed behind him.

"Honestly, I don't know. Everything hurts."

"You are more cognizant today. Yesterday was a bit of a scare for us all."

"I didn't mean to come here," Benjamin told him. "I meant what I said about protecting your family."

"Well, when you wouldn't let Mike take you to the E.R. he decided to bring you over. What are the odds that my partner, and probably the only man who knows we are friends, would be the one to find you."

"It's not odds," Benjamin replied.

"That's what I'm saying, Benjamin. God knew what He was doing when he let Mike bring you here."

"Kara said there was a doctor involved."

Jason glanced at the closed door. "I was pretty clear about that with them."

"It wasn't her fault, Roper. I saw the splint and asked her directly. She's a sweet girl. A lot like you."

"I am not a sweet girl." Jason pretended he was offended.

Benjamin grinned up at him. "So what about the doctor? I thought I was pretty clear on that point. I don't want a paper trail."

"The doctor who saw you is a good friend from our church. We took you in after hours and no reports were made. You were roughed up and a bit loopy. I had to make sure you were okay."

"Thanks."

"Can you tell me what happened?"

"That's what I needed to talk to you about, Roper." Benjamin struggled to sit up

"Lie down," Jason told him. "You can say it from there."

Benjamin lay still. "I don't know who it was."

"What do you mean?"

"Well, the other day, a little weasel guy picked me up at gunpoint and tried to get me to join forces with some mysterious big wig. That made sense. I half expected it."

"You didn't tell me about that."

"Nothing really happened. I gave him a piece of my mind, and he dropped me off by the road." Benjamin glanced at Jason. "That's why I was walking by the park."

"I did wonder, with your leg being hurt and all."

"Thanks for keeping that under your hat, Roper. He was tailing me for a while and I didn't want to take a chance."

"I should be the one thanking you," Jason began.

Benjamin stopped him with a slight lifting of his hand. "Hey, we're friends aren't we?"

"So what about last night?"

"I understand the threats and the gun point stuff. You and I have done all that before." Benjamin frowned. "But last night was different."

"How so?" Jason asked.

"I was just getting ready for bed. I sat down on the bed, took the boot off my foot and wham. Something knocked me right off the bed. I was losing from the start."

"Could you tell how many were there?" Jason moved the bedside lamp to the floor and sat where it had been.

"That's just it. Whoever it was kept striking so hard and fast that I didn't have a chance to react. I didn't even have time to hit the floor before the next blow came. It wasn't like they were trying to take me. They were just striking." Benjamin stared up at the ceiling. "I was totally helpless, Roper. There was nothing I could do. It was like I was in a dryer with a dozen bowling balls banging around me. I couldn't keep up with what was happening."

"How did you get away?"

"I just kept thinking about my family. I knew I couldn't black out because that would be the end. Honestly, I don't know." Benjamin looked over at his friend. "I prayed a lot too."

Jason waited silently.

"I don't know how I got out of there," Benjamin continued. "I vaguely remember falling down a lot of stairs, the taste of dirt....and the taste of blood. I just kept getting up and trying to move away, but whoever it was wouldn't let me." Benjamin's voice drifted off.

"Whoever it was really knew what they were doing," Jason told him. "The Doctor said it must have been mostly pressure points and surface strikes. After all that, you came away with a few cracked ribs, a broken finger, and a slight concussion."

"But why would they do it?" Benjamin asked. "I don't know anyone around here."

Jason sighed. "I don't know, Benjamin. Unless it was because of me."

"What do you mean?"

"Seems like I bring that on you. Word gets out that I know you, and you take the heat because they know you feel it."

"That's not true."

"No?" Jason folded his arms. "That's what I do. You've lived a normal life for the last ten years, right? No fighting, no killing, no hold ups, just the quiet normal stuff. You have a family, you have a job."

"Roper…"

Jason looked away, his jaw muscles working. "Then you come close to me and all hell breaks loose."

"That's not true," Benjamin repeated.

"You stood with me, through the years." Jason was not really talking to Benjamin anymore. "You got shot, you got hurt, and you saved my neck on a number of occasions. What did I do for you, other than curse you by association?"

"This is not about you, Roper," Benjamin informed him. "You've had a tough week."

"Hmm." Jason knew he was being irrational.

"Okay, a tough year," Benjamin corrected. "But think this through rationally. It is not like we have been openly hanging out. I've only been here about a month. And for your information the last ten years haven't exactly been smooth sailing. So don't get bent out of shape and drag up a bunch of stuff you should have dealt with before now."

"You're right." Jason would not have taken this from many people, but he knew Benjamin was right. "I'm sorry."

"Good. Now let's get this hold up sorted out. We know the first guys got their dirt from Seth."

"The Blandy boy?"

"Yes. I don't know how they swung it, but they got in and got him to spill what he knew about my past. It wasn't much, but apparently it was enough to catch their interest."

"Maybe this time was more of a warning," Jason observed thoughtfully. "Kind of a payback for jailing their man."

"How was I supposed to know it was their man?" Benjamin asked wearily. "He's the one who started it at the hotel."

"And without a description we don't have much to go on," Jason pointed out.

"Sorry, next time I'll try to make a sketch." Benjamin promised sarcastically.

Jason frowned at him. "That's not what I was saying."

Benjamin smiled. "Relax a little. If your emotions are tangled your mind will be too. You've got a lot going on in there."

"By the way you also lost a tooth," Jason observed dryly to change the subject.

Benjamin felt with his tongue. "At least it is on the side. After all one tooth isn't so bad. I'm pretty sure I have all the rest of me."

Jason shook his head. "You are an incurable optimist."

Benjamin laughed, and then groaned. "I think I just got cured."

"Maybe I should go see Seth."

"He's still pretty sore at you, Roper. I don't know if that is a good idea."

Jason got up and went to the door. "Just the same, I think I'll give it a try."

TWELVE

"Hey Scott, do you have a minute?" Jason asked from the doorway.

"Um…Sure, Roper. Come on in." Andrew Scott had a habit of calling people by their last names. He said it was a habit he picked up in the Navy. He was a thick bear of a man with graying hair and a neat goatee. He got up and offered his big hand to Jason. "You haven't stopped by in a while. "What's up?"

Jason shook his hand and gave Scott a paper. "I've got another case going on the side and was wondering if you could pull up anything on this boy."

"Seth Blandy." Scott looked it over thoughtfully. "That's the boy you brought in about a month ago right?"

"That's right."

"And you wanted me to run another report?" Scott flipped the paper to see if there was anything else on the back.

"No, I want you to search for him again. Just by description, or split up the name or something. Things keep leading back to him, and I want to find out why."

"So you want an alias or something?"

"Maybe. Is there a way you can pull up his family history or something like that?"

Scott shook his head. "Not unless there was some criminal activity. What you need is a genealogy record, not a police record."

"I'll look into that. Thanks."

"Do you still want me to run this?" Scott tapped the paper.

"If you have time. A name change, parent's marriage, or divorce record. Anything would be helpful at this point."

Scott nodded thoughtfully. "I'll make time."

———

Seth flipped idly through the little New Testament Benjamin had given him. He was worn out from the enforced exercise, and bored enough to try anything. Why hadn't that old counselor showed up? What was so important that he had skipped out without an explanation?

Remembering Benjamin's limp, Seth pondered that for a while. What did a counselor do during his off hours? He flipped a few more pages.

"You shall not steal…I was daily…then after about… the word which God," Seth was reading wherever his eye fell as he let the pages flutter by. "Render therefore….for when they say…for in this manner….sing praises….hear my voice."

"Cut it out will you?"

Seth looked over at his cell mate. "What's it to you?" he asked belligerently.

"Just read the stupid book. Or put it down." The guy was bigger and more muscular than Seth. Word had gotten around that Seth's cell mate was a fierce fighter. Having no desire to find out, Seth backed down.

"Okay, no big deal." Seth opened the pages at random and, with a quick glare at the kill joy, he started reading.

———

"Is everything in order?"

"Not exactly." The single lamp cast hard shadows across the man's weasely face. His thin sharp nose and sunken cheeks gave him an eerie look.

"What do you mean, Fisher?" Thick brows came together above piercing gray eyes.

Fisher shifted. "Adam lost him."

The boss was not impressed. "How could you lose him, he was alone in the room. There were two of you."

"I didn't lose him." Adam had entered the room in time to overhear the accusation. He glared at Fisher. Adam, in sharp contrast to the weasely man beside him, looked as if he had stepped out of an army poster. His shirt sleeves were tight around his thick upper arms, and his casual bearing could not conceal the practiced control of an expert fighter. "You said rough him up. That's what I did," Adam informed him coldly. "You didn't say anything about bringing him in."

"Hmm."

"I did my job, so cough up the dough," Adam pressured. "I don't like this joint."

"Too scary for you, Adam?" The gray eyes were locked on him.

"I did what you asked, and I did it well." Adam did not flinch before the head man as Fisher had done. "All I want is my pay."

The man considered him a moment before pulling a thick envelope from his pocket. "There may be more of this coming your way."

"I choose my own work, Farley," Adam answered, flipping through the bills to insure he had received the full amount. "I didn't care for the company on this job."

Farley's laugh sounded hollow in the empty room. "I'll see what I can do about that."

———

Jason stepped aside to allow his family to file in between the rows of chairs. This was their row in the big sanctuary. It put Jason close to the back where there would not be many people behind him and at the same time gave him a good view of the doors.

An elderly man, whose black hair was graying at the temples, came over to greet them.

"Hello, Doctor Lewis." Jason shook his hand. "How's your week going?"

The doctor tipped his hand from side to side. "Dis week has been not good, not bad. As you say 'so so.'"

"I sure appreciate the favor you did us." Jason meant it.

Doctor Lewis smiled. "You have often done favors for me."

"Yeah, but I owe you big time for this one."

"Perhaps I will collect on it someday," Lewis joked. "It is good to see you, Miss Ellen. You are doing well?"

"Yes, Doctor. How is your wife?"

Again the doctor indicated with the tipping of his hand. "Dis week has been hard on her. De cancer is… it is not good."

"I am sorry to hear that." Ellen retrieved the bulletin from Levi's mouth. "Tell her we are praying for her."

"She will be Tankful."

Someone began a song on the piano and, as if on cue, people started finding their seats.

"I need to talk to you, after." Doctor Lewis motioned with his head toward the front. "It is about de favor."

"Okay, I'll find you after the service."

"What do you think he wants?" Ellen asked in a whisper when Jason sat beside her.

"I don't know." Jason watched as Lewis found his seat. "I guess we will find out."

———

Benjamin sat on the bed waiting for the room to stop spinning. With careful measured movements he got to his feet, keeping his weight on his good leg. His bad ankle was now incased in a hard cast.

He reached across to his phone and typed in a number. He would have to hurry, Roper's church would let out any time.

"Eddie, is that you?"

"Who is this?" Eddie Shartell asked warily.

"This is Benjamin Curr. I need your help."

...he had done to his phone ... With much of the
...could fight with ... whisper ... could not at any time
... "Okay, let me ..."
..."What are you ..." Clark asked ... she does ...
... it ... her mind ... I wonder ...

THIRTEEN

"Do we need to go somewhere where we can talk?" Jason asked when he found Doctor Lewis after church.

"No, I will tell you quickly what I know."

They moved out of the main press. People usually stayed and visited for a good hour after service so this side conversation would not raise suspicion like an outside meeting.

"I have seen one oder patient dis year wid similar injuries to dose of your friend," The doctor confided. "I only tell you dis because you are an officer as well as a friend."

"Who was it?"

"I cannot recall de name, but I will look up de case tomorrow, and tell you den."

"How recently did you see him?"

"Not long, maybe two, tree months past. I remembered it after you had gone." Doctor Lewis put a hand on Jason's arm. "De man, like your friend was not all dere in the head when I see him. He continued to struggle and to repeat, 'Farley' until I sedated him for his own good. I do not know who Farley is, but de basic injuries were, as I said, very similar to your friend. I do not know what happened to dat man."

"Thank you, Doctor. Did you contact the police?"

"No, dough I see now I should have. De little man wid him, he had a vedy pointed nose, it was vedy skinny. Anywho, he said Farley had been de man's dog dat had been hit by a car. I do not know if dis is true. Dat is why I tell you. You follow it and let me know if anyting comes up."

————

"Here is the report you asked for, Roper." Scott held out a thin stack of paper. He went on as Jason thumbed through the sheets. "There's not much there. Mostly petty crimes but I had a little time over the weekend."

A smile slid across Jason's face. "What did you find?"

Scott picked up another thin stack from his desk. "It seems Seth's father died when he was twelve or thirteen."

Jason waited eagerly for the papers, but Scott was enjoying the telling.

"His mother remarried a year or so after he died. Seth got his first misdemeanor very soon after that."

"What was the new father's name?"

"I couldn't find much on him. His name is…" Scott scanned the paper and turned down the first page to see the second. "Here it is. His name is Peter Farley." Scott saw Jason's startled expression. "You know him?"

"I heard of him, just recently." Jason's mind was rapidly connecting the dots. "Scott, we need to reopen this case."

————

"Is Doctor Lewis in?" Jason asked the secretary urgently.

"No, he…" she glanced up and caught sight of Jason's uniform. "Is something wrong?"

"I don't know. I need to see the doctor immediately."

"He went to have lunch with his wife." She clicked away on her keyboard and her eyes scanned the screen. "She's in room 320. Cancer ward."

"Thanks." Jason turned away from the desk and radioed Mike as he walked. "I am going up to see him. I'll need backup."

"You got it."

Mike fell in beside him as Jason jogged down the long

bare hall.

"If they do something to the doctor…" Jason shook his head. He needed to stay objective.

"Keep it cool, Jason," Mike reminded him. "We don't even know if he is in danger."

"We've got to get that name."

"Wouldn't it be in the records?" Mike asked as they waited for the elevator.

"Probably, but I need to make sure Doctor Lewis is safe. He will be a key witness when this all blows open."

"We hope." Mike Fettly was ever the realist.

The door opened and they crowded in.

"What floor?" a thin nosed man asked politely.

Jason remembered the doctor's description of the man who had come to him. This man, with his thin pointed nose and slight stature, fit perfectly. "Um…"

"You don't know what floor?" Mike hissed.

"Where are you going?" Jason asked.

"Three." The man looked nervous.

"That is where we are going." Jason could not take his eyes off him. He had to memorize every feature.

"Have I met you somewhere?" the little man asked uncomfortably.

"I think so. What was your name?"

"Fi…" he reconsidered, "rank."

"Firank?" Mike asked.

"Frank," Fisher corrected. "You know, like honest, frank."

"I guess I had you mixed up with someone else." Jason put his arm out to keep the door open on the third floor. "After you."

"Thank you." Fisher stepped out and then patted his pocket. "Oh dear, I left the card in the car. I'll have to run down and get it."

"That's too bad." Neither believed him.

"Good day." Fisher traded places with them and the doors closed.

"Odd," Mike commented.

"Very. Get Graham to tail him and radio the station. I want someone guarding this room."

"Right." He moved away from the door and Jason faintly heard him repeating Graham's call number.

Jason knocked lightly on the door of room 320.

"Come in?"

Jason removed his hat and pushed the door open. "Doctor Lewis? It's me, Jason." He shut the door lightly behind him.

"Jason! What brings you here?" Doctor Lewis set aside his lunch and rose to meet him. "Margie dear, it's Jason Roper from church."

"Hello, Mrs. Lewis." Jason looked at the pale lady tucked neatly beneath the covers. Tubes and wires draped from the bed to the blinking, beeping machines by the wall. "I don't mean to interrupt."

She gave him a little smile and whispered, "Sit down."

"I'm sorry, I can't stay." Jason looked at the doctor. "I need to talk to you. It will only take a minute."

"Be right back, Margie." Doctor Lewis joined Jason in the little doorway alcove. "What is it?"

"I don't want to scare you, Doctor. But I am afraid you may be in danger."

"What kind of danger?" Lewis asked quietly with a furtive glance toward the bed.

"Did you find the name of the man? The one you told me about Sunday."

"Yes, I was going to call you dis afternoon. Margie has to have her meals right on time."

"I understand." Jason tried not to seem rushed. "What was his name?"

"Now let me see..." Lewis searched the air.

There was a light rap on the door. "We've got company."

"Take your time." Jason was fairly bursting with urgency, but he knew rushing the doctor would only muddle his thinking.

Jason put a hand on his shoulder and gently moved him into the entryway of the little bathroom. "This is a better thinking spot."

"Hmm?" Lewis was confused.

"Just think of the name. The door's here. I don't want you to get hit."

"How many?" Jason asked softly into the radio.

"Weasel brought a very impressive friend," came Mike's answer.

"How are we doing on backup?" Jason retrieved the chair from the far side of the room with a polite "excuse me" to Mrs. Lewis.

"Do I have space to come out?" Jason asked.

"They haven't rounded the corner," Mike replied. "I was down on that end when I saw them."

Jason looked over at the doctor who stood frozen in the bathroom doorway. "Don't worry about it. We've got you covered. Just think of the name." He pulled the door open and slipped into the hall. "Get in there and keep them covered," Jason ordered.

"What about you?" Mike asked.

"Don't worry about me. Just keep them safe. And get a lockdown on this floor. We don't want any guests." Jason stepped away from the door as he spoke. "We need that name. I'm pretty sure at this point they will have pulled the record. I've got a chair by the door to reinforce the lock. Mike, you gotta get that name out of him. "

"I'll do what I can. Be careful." Mike disappeared into the room.

Fourteen

Jason moved quickly down the hall locking the room doors as he went. He was halfway up the opposite side when they rounded the corner.

Mike had been right. The newcomer was seriously impressive. He was not taller than Jason, but he was considerably larger.

"Can I help you?" Jason was still locking the doors as he moved toward them. His experienced eye picked out the slight bulge of a concealed weapon. "Keep them down," he muttered into his radio.

"Maybe," Fisher answered. "We are here to visit Mrs. Lewis."

"I'm sorry, she is not accepting visitors at this time. I can tell her you came by."

"I don't think you understand..."

"Drop it," the big man commanded irritably. "We both know why we are here."

"You both know, or you and I both know?" Jason was buying time.

Adam was not impressed. "I was planning this a little differently."

"To catch him on the walk to his car tonight?" Jason asked.

"Something like that." Adam was sizing up the room and his opposition.

Jason took a shot in the dark. "You roughed up Ethen

Puller and got him to do the bank job, but you didn't think he would be able to keep it quiet."

Fisher's eyes widened and he glanced up at his body guard. "He already talked."

Adam shoved him away. "You mean you talked." Adam was disgusted. "So now you are in this too."

"When Seth was caged, your big man was afraid he would spill to the counselor, so you had to rough him up too."

Adam moved toward him. "Any other last words?"

"Why didn't you tell Benjamin why you were attacking him?" Jason backed away slowly. The stairwell was at the end of the hall so he was not overly concerned.

"I don't know what you are talking about," Adam lied, still coming toward Jason.

"Is that why Seth had a death wish at the cliff? He was afraid of you?"

"You got in a little too deep, Copper." With amazing swiftness Adam closed the distance between them and sent Jason sprawling on the floor. Jason was stunned. Not by the blow but by the speed of it. Adam struck him again and Jason saw his Glock in the big man's hand.

Jason scrambled to his feet as Adam bore down on him. "That was impressive."

Adam jabbed him hard and Jason stumbled a little. That was how he had done it. This guy was some kind of pressure point expert. Jason did his best to flee to the stairs, but somehow Adam was always right on top of him, always knocking him off balance.

Just as fast as he had attacked he was gone. "Mike get away from the door," Jason warned. He reached for his taser but it was gone too. "You are really fast." He could not help marveling.

There was a flicker of pride on Adam's face. He backed up a few steps and pointed Jason's Glock at the Lewis' room door.

"I already know what you are trying to keep quiet," Jason reminded him. "Leave them alone. Doctor Lewis doesn't know about any of this."

"I like to keep things tidy," Adam informed him. His face was hard as he sent three shots through the door of 320.

Jason didn't hear anyone cry out. He licked his lips nervously. "Now what?"

"Now I take you with me." Adam's face was still hard. "Or else I stay here and see how long it takes me to hit someone in there."

"Okay. I come with you and you leave them alone."

The edge of Adam's mouth turned up a little.

"See, that thing you just did didn't look like a yes." Jason had a hand on the stairwell door, but he knew he couldn't leave Mike and the Lewis' unprotected. This guy was too fast, too well trained, and Jason knew he did not have a chance against him. All he could do was keep buying time. But what would time do? Jason wondered. Would more officers do any good?

Jason walked toward him slowly but steadily. "I want my gun back."

"I bet you do." Adam fired another shot through the door. "But I suggest you keep your distance."

"So, we are at a stalemate." Jason stood where he was.

"Not exactly. I am taking all three of you with me."

"Three?"

"Your partner in the room. Did you think I was that stupid?" Adam sent another bullet into the room and swapped to his own weapon. "Toss me your extra clip."

Jason took it out slowly.

"Toss it." Adam ordered putting the barrel of his gun against the door and angling it toward where the bed would be.

Jason tossed it and he caught it easily.

"Now call off your backup."

Jason pressed the radio. "All vehicles be advised, I have a hostage situation. All officers are to pull out from the hospital grounds. I repeat, I have a hostage situation, clear the grounds and the surrounding area." Jason locked eyes with Adam. "Happy?"

"Fisher."

The little man appeared from around the corner. He looked scared.

"Get the cuffs off his belt and get his hands behind his back."

Fisher hurried to obey but Adam's hand on his chest stopped him short.

"Get the key. And Fisher, don't mess this up."

Fisher was sweating. It ran down into his eyes as he unsnapped the cuffs. He paused to wipe his eyes and Jason grabbed the cuffs and snapped one on Fisher's wrist. He was vaguely aware of the sound of a bullet as he spun Fisher around and secured his remaining wrist.

Another bullet. Jason felt it strike, the impact caused him to step back a little. This guy was using heavy ammo.

"Seth was right." Adam had not meant to say it aloud.

Jason glared at him. "You picked the wrong guy to work for."

Adam's eyes narrowed. He raised the gun and fired. Fisher cried out and wilted beside him. Jason let him fall. Adam sent a second shot into Jason's radio. The bullet struck his shoulder and jerked him backward. Jason quickly righted himself.

"I'm going to disappear," Adam told Jason, his gaze steady. "You have a nice thing here, so I will pull out and leave Farley to you. You come after me, and I'll spill your secret. If you forget this, so will I."

"What about him?" Jason gestured at the body at his feet. "What about Ethen Puller?"

Adam did not respond.

"You are in too deep to walk away now," Jason informed him bluntly.

"There is only one other option," Adam informed him. "I follow you."

Jason frowned. "What does that mean?"

"Wherever you go, I'll find you and I'll expose your little secret. Or…" Adam paused for effect. "you forget you ever saw me and life resumes as normal."

Jason shook his head. "You made the choice to take up with this outfit, and you are going to have to take what comes with it."

Adam's smile was cold. "That's what you think." He walked toward Jason. "Get this straight. I'm going to shoot anyone I see on the way out. I don't care who it is, or what they are doing. If I see them, they're dead. Got it?"

Jason knew he meant it. "I can't instantly clear the whole hospital." Jason objected as panic welled up inside. "You've got to give me time to…"

Adam's huge fist sent him sprawling to the floor.

Jason scrambled to his feet. "Give me five minutes and I'll clear it…" He hurriedly backed away, but his heel hit Fisher's body and he fell, trying hard to avoid Fisher's body.

Adam grabbed the front of Jason's uniform and jerked him to his feet. "I'm a nice guy." Adam sneered in Jason's face. "I'll give you two minutes."

Propelled by Adam's powerful shove he stumbled down the hall. In a moment Jason had his footing, and he ran the remaining distance to the desk.

"This is the police," Jason announced over the loudspeaker. "Everyone clear the halls. We are instating an emergency lockdown. This is not a drill. Wherever you are, get out of sight, if you are in an open area your life is in danger. I repeat, this is not a drill. This hospital is under a lockdown.

Get out of the halls…"

Jason switched off the loudspeaker. "Lord, help them," he whispered.

Grabbing the phone Jason dialed 911.

"Nancy this is Jason. I need a chopper over the hospital, now."

Jason heard her radio the helicopter.

"What's going on, Jason?"

"There is a killer in this hospital. I need the chopper to verify when he leaves. There are a lot of lives at stake."

"They are already in the air, so they should be over that area any minute."

"Get a call in to the juvenile detention center. The Blandy kid may be next. And Nancy?"

"Yes?"

"Could you send someone by my house?"

"I can do that."

Jason hung up and ran for the stairs. Adam was waiting for him just around the corner.

Jason attempted to dodge the big hand that shot towards him, but only managed to lessen the impact.

"So you called for a chopper?" Adam asked shoving him up against the wall.

"I had to know when you were out." Jason squirmed to lessen the pressure on his windpipe.

"I'm not out," Adam hissed.

"You can use me," Jason told him quickly. "No one else knows. You can put the gun to my head and walk out."

"No one knows?" Adam pressed harder and Jason could feel the man's hot breath.

"No one on the force. Everyone else should be out already."

Adam thought it over for a long moment.

"Alright." Adam spun him around and his thick arm encircled Jason's neck. Jason tucked his chin to control the constriction. With the steady pressure of the gun barrel on his temple Jason moved forward with his captor. They took the elevator down, and walked through the lobby without seeing a soul.

Jason kept his eyes straight ahead, praying every step of the way.

The helicopter whirred by, flying low and Adam pulled Jason back inside.

"Call them off. Tell them to land," Adam demanded, shoving him at the front desk.

Jason rounded the desk cautiously. The receptionist was huddled beneath it. Jason put his hand out to stop her, and she crouched lower.

Jason made the call and they waited. The helicopter made one last pass and then flew due south. Jason came out from behind the desk and they watched it disappear.

"Alright, you." He grabbed the collar of Jason's uniform and pressed the gun in his side. "Start marching."

Jason went quietly. He was surprised to see the sun still high in its arch. It felt like a lifetime had passed since he had first walked through the hospital door.

Adam guided him to a beat up SUV that was parked in the side lot. "Get down on the grass."

Jason obeyed, laying face down in the warm grass.

"You count to a thousand real slow got it? Once you get there you can get up. Not before."

Jason nodded without lifting his head. He could feel the big man staring down at him. He closed his eyes and waited. Finally he heard him walk away and the engine of the SUV revved to life. When Jason could no longer hear the motor, he started counting.

Fifteen

"The Lewis' are fine. A little shook up, but not hurt."

"What about Seth?"

"No one had been there today. They transferred him to a high security cell and reinforcements are on their way from the station on the north side."

"I could kick myself for letting him go." Jason's fingers were laced tightly through his short hair.

"What else could you do?" Graham asked. "Just be grateful he didn't kill you."

Jason did not answer.

"Why don't you go home? You've already done your report, given your statement, and talked to the chief. There's not much else we can do at this point."

"What about Peter Farley?" Jason asked wearily.

"We don't have anything but suspicion on him. The chief is having him tailed for now."

Mike put a hand on Jason' hunched shoulder. "Let me take you home. We've got your house covered."

Jason nodded slowly. "Okay."

Mike took his civilian car so as not to raise suspicion with Jason's neighbors. They were half-way there before Mike spoke.

"There's something I've been meaning to ask you."

"What's that?" The passenger seat was reclined and Jason's eyes were closed.

Mike hesitated so long that Jason turned his head to peer over at him. "Are you going to ask it?"

"I don't know how to put it," Mike confessed.

Jason closed his eyes again. "Just spit it out."

"Are you invincible?"

Jason did not move. "What makes you ask that?"

"I don't know." Mike glanced across at Jason. "I just thought you were really good at what you did."

"And now?"

"The trial got me thinking," Mike told him. "You never directly said the boy didn't shoot you. That struck me as odd. But then I thought about how you feel about lying and all." Mike hesitated. "Do you mind talking about this?"

"You are the one talking," Jason pointed out.

"Well, I got to thinking about how you are always putting yourself in harm's way. And you carry that duffle."

Jason smiled without opening his eyes. "You looked in it didn't you?"

"Yeah I did."

"Anything interesting?" Jason asked mildly.

"There was a uniform and a set of civilian clothes." Mike was embarrassed. "I only looked because…"

"I don't mind, Mike."

"Well this is kind of awkward. You've been my partner for three years, can't you just deny it or something?" Mike flashed his badge at the undercover cop on the corner and pulled to a stop in front of Jason house. Jason did not move.

"Is that what you want?"

"You never get hurt," Mike blurted out. "I just thought you were lucky, but now…"

"Now you think I am invincible."

"I heard all the shots in the hall today. He couldn't have missed you that often."

"No, he couldn't."

"Jason you are making this very difficult."

"Actually, Mike, you are." Jason found the lever and sat the seat up. "Like you said. I've been your partner for three years. I'm not going to lie to you."

"Well then, are you invincible?" Mike asked again.

"I am."

Mike stared at him in disbelief.

Jason looked out the windshield. "If you can keep it to yourself, I would appreciate it."

Mike was still staring.

Jason glanced at him and laughed "I feel like I just grew horns or something."

"I'm sorry. You really are invincible?"

"Yes."

"I don't believe it." Mike was now staring out the windshield. "After three years."

"I hope you understand why I didn't tell you. It is kind of a security measure I have to take."

"The bank robber shot you didn't he?"

"Yes, he did."

"And that maniac at the grocery store last month. You stopped his bullet when you got in front of me."

"Yes. Mike, I would have told you if you needed to know."

"Yeah but, wow. Is there anything else I should know?"

Jason smiled. "I don't think so."

"Totally invincible?" Mike asked.

"Mike, now that you know, or really, now that the big guy knows. Um… you do realize this means I have to move on."

"You mean quit the force?"

"I mean literally move on. Once it gets out, my name goes viral and people start coming out of the woodwork to try me out. Then they start hurting the people near to me, trying to break me that way. It is not good for my family to have me always on edge and defensive. I've got to find

95

Fisher's friend before he finds my family."

"Benjamin knows?"

"Yes, he knows."

"And Ellen?"

"She knew before she married me."

"Wow." Mike leaned his head back on the headrest. "This has been a crazy day."

Jason's laugh sounded empty and sad. "Go home and get some rest." He opened the door and got out. "I'll let you know before I leave for good."

———

Seth began back pedaling the moment he saw Jason.

"I'm not going in there with that freak of nature," he yelled trying to push past the guard. Instead, he found himself roughly shoved into the chair.

"Don't give him any trouble." The guard stalked out of the room leaving them alone.

"Hello, Seth."

Seth glared at the surface of the table. Refusing to acknowledge the officer on the other side existed.

"I understand you not wanting to meet with me." Jason laid a manila folder on the table. "But there are some things I need you to look at."

"You aren't getting any help from me, Freak," Seth blurted. He knew the guard would be on top of him in a second if he got up, so he sat and seethed.

"Have you seen this man?" Jason laid a picture of Ethen Puller on the table and Seth diverted his eyes. "Or this one?" He set Fisher's picture beside it.

"That is why you wanted me to drop you when you were hanging over the cliff, isn't it. You were afraid you would get what they got."

"I'm not afraid." Seth's tone was hateful.

"Ethen and Fisher were both shot because they messed up. They got caught, and that's not allowed."

Seth did not respond.

"The only problem was, they couldn't get to you."

Seth's eyes met Jason's for only an instant.

"But they were scared. They didn't know if you had what it took to keep quiet. So they roughed up your friend to make sure you wouldn't spill the beans."

"I don't know what you are talking about."

"No?" Jason laid a third picture on the table. "Does the name Benjamin ring a bell?"

Seth looked in spite of himself. He was shocked to see his counselor with a swollen face and black eye.

"What did you do to him?" Seth demanded. "He didn't do anything."

"I didn't do it, Seth," Jason answered evenly. "Do you remember the last time he came to see you?"

"Yeah, he had a limp. Said some creep tried to jump him."

"When it didn't work the first time, they came back and knocked him around to keep him from coming to see you."

"It worked," Seth pouted. "Skipped out like a pansy."

"You call that a pansy?" Jason tapped the picture. "That limp you talked about was a fractured bone. He came here before getting it checked out in case it was something that would keep him away."

"So?"

"So, Mr. Blandy. Your life is in danger."

"They can't touch me."

"You knew it on the cliff. That is why you tried to kill me. You knew falling a hundred feet would be better than meeting your father's thugs."

"He's not my father." The bitterness in his voice did not surprise Jason.

"But he married your mother."

"That doesn't make him my father," Seth countered. "My dad died."

"I understand you feeling that way, Seth. I had a run in with someone your...Mr. Farley was paying. I don't mind saying, I was scared to death. I don't know who he was but I am glad your counselor made it out alive."

"That's Adam." Seth did not look up. "He's Farley's favorite."

"Do you know his last name?" Jason knew he was taking a chance.

Seth shook his head. "He never gives it. He's a freelance fighter. The only one Farley can't control." He added with a touch of pride.

"Seth, Farley is gunning for you. I need you to tell me everything you know. Your life depends on it."

Sixteen

"You shot Fisher," Peter Farley stated as soon as Adam entered the bare room.

"You got a problem with that?" Adam demanded. "I told you I didn't like the company."

"I didn't pay you to shoot him."

"You didn't pay me at all," Adam corrected coolly. "You give me a couple grand, and I'll clear out."

"And if I don't?"

Adam folded his thick arms across his chest. "Maybe I'll stick around."

"You didn't finish the Lewis job."

"Your little man screwed that one up," Adam pointed out. "Or was it your idea to go inside and get spotted by every security guard on the grounds?"

"So you want me to cover for you while you skip town." Farley leaned his chair until his back rested against the wall. "But Adam, you forgot to finish the job."

Adam's sweep kick pulled the chair out from under Farley and he crashed to the floor. "I don't think you understood me the first time, Farley." Adam grabbed him by the lapels and shoved him against the wall. "I said give me a couple of grand and I'll clear out."

Adam saw the fear in the man's once piercing gray eyes.

"You win. I'll give you the money."

Adam released him and, with a quick jab, crumpled him

to the floor. Farley tried to get to his feet and Adam dropped him again. This time he deftly swiped the handgun from beneath Farley's suit coat. On his hands and knees, Farley took a moment to recover.

"I said I'll give you the money." There was a hint of a plea in his tone.

"I'm waiting." Adam had folded his arms again.

Farley got to his feet a bit unsteadily and slid his hand into his coat. "I can still use you…" With a sudden jerk, he looked up at Adam.

"Missing something?" Adam asked without moving.

"No." Farley knew he was beaten.

"I'm not a very patient man, Farley," Adam warned.

Farley pulled his hand from the empty holster under his jacket and took a thick envelope from his pocket. "This was your pay for the Lewis job."

"Is that all you have?" Adam let him hold it out. Enjoying the slight tremble of the tyrant's hand.

Farley felt his pockets and came up with another grand.

"I guess that will do." Adam took it all and shoved it into his pocket. "Now I'll keep my end and clear out." Adam narrowed his eyes. "You wouldn't be dumb enough to try anything, but it doesn't hurt to be safe. So get down on the floor and start counting…"

———

"You alright?" Ellen asked stepping over Jason's legs.

He was sprawled on his back in the living room floor.

"I think I am." Jason smiled up at her. "It just feels good to lie here."

Benj came in and assessed the situation. "I want to feel." He flopped down next to Jason peering over to make sure he was lying the same way.

"So is it all cleared up?" Ellen sat on the couch and tucked her feet under her. She had one of Kara's dresses to mend.

"No. This Adam guy is still out there. Ellen, he's a scary character."

"He looks scary?" Ellen asked trying a second time to thread her needle.

"That's just it, he doesn't. He's about my height, but really in shape. I mean like the poster man for in shape people."

Ellen laughed.

"It's not funny, El. You should have seen the guy. He was just strolling along toward me and wham I was on the floor."

"Is that why you are on the floor?" Benj asked sitting up. "Did somebody hit you?"

"No, Benj, I just wanted to lie here." Jason tussled the little boy's hair. "I was telling Mommy what happened yesterday."

"Oh."

Ellen looked up as if seeing her son for the first time. "What are you doing up?"

"I just wanted to lay here with Daddy," Benj answered innocently.

"Well, I suggest you move yourself back to your bed." She cocked her head toward the hall.

He scrambled up looking down at Jason with pleading eyes.

"Mommy gave you an instruction, Benj." Jason reminded him.

Benj gave Ellen a hug to give them time to change their minds. When they did not invite him to stay, he sighed and trudged out of the room.

"Good night, Benj," Jason called after him.

"Goodnight," he mumbled back.

"How is Benjamin?" Jason asked folding his hands behind his head.

"He seems okay. I was kind of busy today with all the Christmas planning."

"It's still two months away." Jason rolled over and propped himself on his elbow. "We still need to talk about moving."

Ellen groaned. "I'm not looking forward to that."

"I know. I'm not either. But hey, three years is pretty good."

Ellen laughed. "I guess military families do it pretty close to that."

"Well, well, look what the cat drug in," Jason announced as Benjamin hobbled into the living room. He paused to look at them and then limped across to the recliner and sat down gingerly.

"We were just talking about you."

"We were talking about moving," Ellen reminded Jason. Her eyes sparkled at him and an amused smile tugged at the edges of her mouth.

"We talked about him before that." Jason looked over at Benjamin. "Why are you prowling around this late at night?"

"It's nine," Benjamin answered. "I'm a big boy now and can stay up until ten."

Jason grinned. Graham and James had picked up Farley at his house about an hour ago. For Jason, it was as if a weight had been lifted from him. Even though the case was not closed, Jason felt like celebrating.

"How's your family?" Ellen asked Benjamin.

"They are doing well. Brook, that's my wife, was a little shook up by it all, but she's okay."

"And the kids?"

Benjamin smiled. "They were happy and loud."

Jason could tell Benjamin wished he were with them.

"What is this about your moving?" Benjamin asked. "Did the cat get out of the bag?"

Jason ran his hand over his face. "In a manner of speaking."

"Which manner?"

Jason looked at Ellen. "I was going to tell you a little more gently."

"Sorry," Benjamin muttered.

Jason could tell he did not mean it. "Thanks, Benjamin."

"I'd leave you alone but I don't think I'd make it back down the hall."

"You old coot." Jason got up and went to sit by Ellen. "Ellen, you remember when I told you about Adam?"

"That was five minutes ago, Jason." Ellen laughed "I think that is just a little too gentle."

Jason sighed and glanced at Benjamin. "Adam promises to follow me and, as Benjamin so adequately put it, 'let the cat out of the bag' everywhere I go."

"Oh." Ellen set down her mending. "But he isn't trying to hurt you."

"How can he?" Jason asked. "He knows that would be useless, so he is just going to keep the heat on me wherever I go. I was thinking maybe I should go away for a while, to kind of let this cool over."

"So we wouldn't be in danger?" Ellen asked pointedly.

"Yes." Jason looked down at his hands.

Ellen put her hand on his arm. "For how long?"

Benjamin cleared his throat. "I think this is where I should cut in."

They looked at him expectantly.

"I have arranged a…" Benjamin cleared his throat again. "I'm expecting a friend," he finished lamely.

"So that is why you dragged yourself out here. Anyone I know?"

Benjamin smiled like a child at Christmas. "Guess."

Jason's brow creased in thought.

"Who?" Ellen asked looking from one to the other.

"A friend by the name of Eddie Shartell, Ma'am."

"Eddie!? He's coming here?" Jason got to his feet.

"I thought he could help you," Benjamin answered innocently.

"Help me what?" Jason demanded. "With Eddie comes a whole retinue of who knows what."

"With a guy like Adam after you…"

"Benjamin, people watch people like Eddie. He's got a lot of enemies."

"He's got more friends than enemies, Jason."

"The children are sleeping," Ellen reminded them softly.

The phone rang and Jason scrambled up to get it. "Hello?"

"Hey, Jason. This is Louie." Eddie's voice had not changed much over the years.

"Hey Louie, what's up?" Jason hurried down the hall and into the bathroom where he turned on the shower and sink and let the water run.

"Are you still at the party?"

"Sure. Where should I be?" Jason asked, playing along.

"Won't your landlord be waiting around to kill you if you come in late?"

Jason frowned, Eddie had a good point. Adam was still a very real threat. "You're right, I forgot about her."

"I'm on my way," Eddie informed him. "I'll loan you my car. I plan to sack out there after the party anyway."

"Alright, I'll be ready." Jason turned off the phone and laid it on the bathroom counter. He looked at his reflection in the fogging mirror. Would he ever be able to just be normal? Even as he asked the question he knew it could not be. There was no way out. Even if there was, he had been invincible for too long to go back now. Jason knew that this life was what God had called him to.

"Lord, please protect my family," Jason whispered. He turned off the water and brought the phone back out to where Ellen and Benjamin were waiting.

"Well?" Benjamin asked.

"Ellen, can I talk to you?"

"Sure." She sensed the tension in his voice and followed

him back to the bathroom. Once again he turned on the water as a precaution.

"Ellen, I'm leaving tonight."

"Where will you go?" Ellen asked softly.

"Eddie's got a place set up for me." Jason smiled at her surprised look. "That's Eddie for you. Always two jumps ahead of the pack." Jason's smile faded. "He's afraid Adam will try to get at me tonight. If he did, you and the kids could get hurt as well. We need you to pretend you are having a party. Act like I am going home when I leave."

"Alright."

"I'll be the bait. I will draw him away to where Eddie's team can get at him without innocents being involved."

"Is that what I am? An Innocent?" Ellen asked.

"Yes, my dear Ellen, and ever so much more." Jason put his arms around her and held her tight. "And I will protect you to my very last breath."

"Jason."

He stepped back to look into her eyes.

"I love you for protecting me, and the kids. But God is the one Who ultimately makes the call. If something were to happen to us…"

"Ellen, no."

"Let me finish." Ellen held his hands tightly as she spoke. "If something were to happen to us, it would be God's best, and you would have accept it as such."

He looked away, unable to bear the thought.

"Jason, don't you remember when Kara broke her arm?" Ellen's voice choked and she struggled to continue. "We were right there, when she fell."

A tear slid down her cheek and Jason pulled her close.

Her breath was shaky as she rested her head against him. "Just remember to let God pick you back up and take care of you." She finally whispered.

"I love you, Ellen."

Jason's phone buzzed on the counter beside them. Releasing Ellen, he wiped at his moist eyes and put the phone to his ear.

"A car just pulled up," Benjamin informed them from the living room.

"Thanks." Jason turned off the water and sighed heavily.

"Don't ever forget that I love you." Ellen smoothed the shoulder of Jason's black t-shirt. It was damp from her tears. "No matter what happens, I love you."

"I love you too." Jason looked at her for a long moment.

There was a knock on the door as they entered the living room.

"Be careful," She whispered as he went to open it.

"Hey, Man! How's it going?" Eddie slapped Jason's shoulder. "Your land lady is going to be ticked. You had better get out there quick." The years had been kind to Eddie. A few new wrinkles had been added, but over all, he was just as Jason remembered him.

"Grouchy old lady. I'm a grown man. A cop," Jason complained loudly. "I just can't afford higher rent."

Eddie laughed and shut the door. As if by magic he was suddenly holding a Glock in a concealed holster, and four ammo clips. "These babies might come in handy," he said quietly.

Jason took them without answering. His own Glock was tucked neatly in the cargo pocket holster, so he slid the new gun under his belt and carefully stashed the clips. While he was doing this, Eddie grilled his new apartment address into him. He had Jason repeat it back several times before he was satisfied. "Go through the side gate on the left side of the house. It is lit by a streetlight and you reach over to unlatch it."

"Okay." Jason quickly reviewed the information in his head.

"There is a garage out back." He dug in his pocket. "Here's the key. You get in and go up-stairs. The light switch is also on your left. Turn on the lights and stay close to the window."

"Thanks, Eddie." Jason shook his hand.

"Remember, whatever happens stay by the open window."

Jason nodded and quickly hugged Ellen before opening the door again. He raised his voice to a party level as he stepped out onto the porch. "Thanks for having me, it was a great party!"

"Have a safe trip home." Ellen called after him. There was a deeper message in the simple statement.

"Hey, Jason." Eddie tossed him the keys to the car in the driveway. "You wouldn't have gotten far without those." Everyone laughed.

"Thanks." Jason opened the car door and turned to wave. "Goodnight!"

Seventeen

As a precaution Seth had been moved to a solitary cell with increased security. He had no contact with anyone, except the guard who brought his meals. Before, this would have produced a teenage tantrum, but now Seth appreciated the extra time to think.

He paced slowly, his eyes moving rapidly across the page before him. Seth had run across a little section in the back of the Bible labeled 'I John'. It had struck him as a funny title, as if the man were beginning a pledge. If he had been the author it would have been called "I Seth." He read it for its title, but what he read in that letter both confused and excited him.

Because he was alone Seth read it aloud. "Beloved, let us love one another, for love is of God; and everyone who loves is born of God and knows God. He who does not love does not know God, for God is love." Seth pondered that for a minute. His mom always said she loved him, but she had never had time for him, and had married a creep Seth hated. Seth shook his head. No, that was not love. He thought of his Dad, his real dad. His dad was the only person who had really loved him, not like Farley. Farley only wanted to use him. He promised big things but never cashed in on them. Instead, Seth was in jail paying for it himself.

Seth frowned and read on. "In this the love of God was manifested toward us, that God has sent His only begotten Son into the world, that we might live through Him." He scratched his head and read it again silently. Sitting on the bed Seth tried to take it apart. "God sent His Son so we can live." He was not sure what that meant but that was the basic message he picked out. Still frowning, Seth closed the little book. "That must be some kind of code."

"Hey Guard," Seth called loudly.

"What?" The guard did not come to the door.

"Do you know much about Bibles?"

"Some I guess."

"Do you know what 'In this the love of God was manifested toward us, that God has sent His only begotten Son into the world, that we might live through Him.' means?"

"It's night, why aren't you sleeping?"

"Come on," Seth pressed. "What does it mean?"

"Say it again," The guard muttered.

Seth read it again a little louder.

"I heard a guy on the radio say it like this. 'God loved us and sent His only Son to die in our place.'"

"Yeah, but what does it mean?"

"It means we broke God's law or something and so we had to die or something. But then God decides, 'No, I think I'll let My Boy die instead of that lousy rat.' But there is something about having to take the gift of forgiveness or something. I heard it a while back, I don't really remember that part."

Seth thought about that. Would God really forgive anyone who took the gift? Seth had never considered forgiveness as an option. He just took the slam that came with the job. He was a crook and figured he would always be one. But what if Benjamin had been right? What if there was still a way out. "Did God pay for everyone, or just the church people?"

"Beats me," The guard said through a yawn. "Why don't you sleep on it?"

"How do you take the gift?" Seth pressed.

"Believe or something," came the guard's vague reply.

"I'm a security guard not a preacher."

"Believe or something," Seth repeated to himself softly as the guard walked on.

————

Jason checked the rearview mirror. The same car had been behind him for a long time. It was not the SUV Adam had been driving when he left the hospital, but then Jason had not expected him to keep it. He was too smart for that.

Putting on his blinker, Jason turned off the main road and went around the block. The car did not follow.

"Calm down, Jason," He told himself. "You are half way there." He scanned the street while waiting for the light to change. Traffic was light, which was why Jason had chosen this road. If something happened, he wanted it to be away from people.

The light turned green and Jason resumed his original route. There was a little stretch up ahead where several shopping centers and strip malls lined the main road. Jason prayed he could make it through without incident, but he had a nagging feeling of dread.

Another red light. Jason pulled to a stop and waited.

Traffic started to move but was hampered by a chorus of horns blowing. Jason spotted a medium sized dog that had wandered into the intersection. Knowing he had time before the light would change, Jason hopped out and in a few steps had caught the dog's collar.

"Go home," Jason commanded once he got it to the edge of the road.

The dog, frightened by the noise and lights, was more than willing to lope off into the darkness.

Jason turned in time to see a pair of bright lights bearing down on him. He dove out of the way and scrambled to his feet. A lady screamed and Jason saw the truck was backing toward him rapidly.

Jason managed to dodge the truck again.

It slammed into a car that was still parked in the inter-section. Jason heard the squeal of the tires on the pavement and ran for his life, knowing all the time that he could not outrun the truck. Jason was vaguely aware of a crowd that had gathered on the sidewalk to his right. The truck bumper slammed into Jason and he felt the terrible pressure bear down on him as the tire crossed his upper body. Gasping for breath Jason watched the tail lights of the speeding vehicle disappear.

People were screaming, and shouting. Jason was aware of the faint wail of sirens. He lay still, fighting for the breath that had been crushed out of him.

"He's alive," someone nearby shouted back to the crowd.

"This guy must be made of steel." Someone knelt beside him "That tire went right over him."

"The ambulance is on the way," the first man informed Jason. They were afraid to touch him.

Jason remembered Adam's promise to expose him wher-ever he went. Adam had planned it well.

"Over here." The man waved frantically to the ambulance. The intersection was backed up for miles and the rescue vehicle was having trouble getting through.

Flashing lights lit the pavement and Jason found himself surrounded by paramedics.

"Stop the cameras." Jason kept his face hidden behind his arm.

"Everyone step back," the paramedic commanded. "We need room to work."

"Where do you hurt?" the second paramedic asked gently sliding a neck brace in place.

Jason chose not to answer.

The police arrived and pushed the crowds further back.

An officer directed the fire department's engine and squad car to where they formed a shield around the body.

Jason allowed himself to be gingerly flipped onto a stretcher and loaded into the ambulance.

"What about the other car?" he asked once they had closed the doors.

The paramedics looked at each other in surprise.

"We have an ambulance with them. It did not sound like their injuries were serious."

"Good."

The ambulance pulled out with a pulsating wail and headed for the hospital.

"Would you mind unstrapping me?"

Again they glanced at each other.

"We need to keep you still. Your body has had serious trauma."

"I have had trauma, but not to my body."

"Maybe you feel fine…"

"Don't do that." Jason saw the paramedic was preparing an IV. "I don't do needles."

"You won't even feel it."

"That's the problem." Jason looked up at the ceiling and worked his hand with difficulty into his back pocket and slid out his badge. "I'm from the police. Let me off of this gurney."

"Sir, I understand your credentials usually get you past a lot of opposition. But here…" the paramedic glanced at his partner who nodded him to go on. "You just got run over by a truck. There are certain reactions people have to extreme trauma like this."

"Okay," Jason sighed. "How do I say this without trauma-tizing you for life? It really would help if you would unstrap me. I think better when I am not strapped down."

The man with the IV mouthed "head trauma". The other paramedic nodded sadly.

"I just don't want you to blab it all over town," Jason continued. "I usually keep it kind of to myself. But in this situation, since this is why he ran me over."

"You know who did it?"

"Yes. He wanted my…secret to be public."

They looked at him with confused expressions. "What secret."

"Unstrap me and I will tell you." Jason was annoyed. He despised the feeling of forced confinement. "I'm not in pain. Just let me off this stretcher. I feel like I am being kidnapped."

"Go ahead and do it," the paramedic told his partner. "It's better to keep him quiet." He stashed the IV and helped undo the last strap.

Jason sat up and swung his legs off the side of the stretcher. The driver swerved a little and Jason knew he had seen him through the little window.

The paramedics' reactions were completely opposite. One jumped back with a yell of fear. The other simply stared at Jason with the slightest frown.

"I don't know how to break it gently," Jason told them, removing the neck brace. "I'm invincible."

"Cool."

Jason could not help smiling at the younger man's reaction.

"I would really appreciate it if you all could keep this under your hats for a while," Jason continued. "I'm sure you can see why this would be necessary."

"All the super heroes have to do it," the younger man informed his partner. "Otherwise the bad guy messes with all the little people who the hero likes."

"Something like that," Jason agreed. "So, will you help me out and keep this quiet?"

"Sure." The paramedic was still staring at Jason with a puzzled expression of awe. "After all, who would believe us?"

They dropped Jason off a few blocks from the address

Eddie had given him. He did not want to take any chances by giving them the real address. Jogging quickly, Jason wove his way through the dimly lit neighborhood. The houses were spaced by plentiful lawns and Jason knew that this was why Eddie had picked the house he did.

The house was an old one story job, but it had been kept neat over the years. The side gate was bigger than Jason had expected. It was low enough to reach over but wide enough for a car to drive through. The driveway curved through the gate and disappeared into the dim outline of the garage behind the house. Jason let himself in through the gate as instructed. There was a dark stretch between the gate and the garage and he hesitated a moment before moving forward.

Eighteen

He was halfway to the garage when the motion sensing light came to life. Adam stood before him, a hard silhouette against the bright light. His shadow stretched out toward Jason, making him seem all the more intimidating.

"That was a nice set up today," Jason commented walking toward the big man.

"I'm glad you liked it." Adam was not smiling.

"It worked out very nicely." Jason stopped. "Now I would like to go up to my room."

"Go ahead."

The way he said it sent chills up Jason's spine.

"You said you were going to expose me, not stalk me," Jason reminded him, keeping his voice steady as he walked forward.

"Maybe I changed my mind." Adam lashed out and Jason stumbled from the impact. Adam's foot hooked Jason's ankle and sent him to the ground.

"Take out your guns and lay them on the pavement where I can see them."

'Why didn't I shoot him?" Jason groaned inwardly. "I had a clear shot, what is wrong with me." Adam was so intimidating that Jason had been more focused on escaping than he had been on stopping the big man. Now, Jason had no choice but to obey. Adam kicked the guns away as Jason laid them down.

"Alright get up." Adam commanded once he had picked up both guns.

"I don't have money," Jason told him.

"How about upstairs?" Adam did not wait for him to respond. "Start walking."

Jason gave him plenty of room as he made his way to the door. "I don't think there's much up there, but I'll give you whatever I can find."

"Let's hope you find a lot."

Jason felt for the light and switched it on. There was an old town car parked in the garage and a few shelves lined with odds and ends. He did not stop to look around, but hurried up the stairs to the room above. The light switch was right where Eddie had said. Jason walked quickly across the room. There were two windows, both on the side toward the house. They were widely spaced, leaving only about a foot between the window and adjoining walls. One had been covered with a heavy drape. The far window, however, was open, it had only a thin sheer curtain that ruffled gently in the cool breeze. Jason went to the desk under the far window and pulled open the middle drawer. There were three one hundred dollar bills stashed inside. Beside them lay a handgun.

Jason hesitated. "Is three hundred enough?"

"What do you think?" Adam demanded.

"It's all I have." Jason's hand closed around the butt of the gun. "Do you want it or not?" he glanced over his shoulder at Adam who was glaring at him from across the room.

Jason took the money with his left hand and turned to face Adam. His gun barked twice and Adam jerked with the impact but did not fall. Instead, he returned fire disabling the handgun before Jason could get off another round.

"Did you think I would be stupid enough to come without protection?" Adam was furious.

Jason backed against the desk, the money falling unheeded to the floor. Adam charged him and Jason stood his ground. Adam barreled into him, slamming him against the wall. Heaving Jason away from the window Adam tossed him into the middle of the room. He followed up, venting his anger by beating Jason down each time he rose.

Jason had only one goal, to stay by the window. Again and again he forced himself to sprint back to the desk beneath the window. Each time it was a little harder to get up. Praying hard, Jason raised himself for what seemed like the hundredth time. He took one step and Adam's hand struck his neck sending him down face first. He lay for a moment, catching his breath.

"Had enough?" Adam asked walking around Jason. He stood towering over Jason with his back to the window.

"Yes," Jason mumbled raising himself to his knees. He hoped the humble answer would buy him time.

Adam strode over to Jason and heaving him to his feet by the front of his torn jacket. "What were you trying to get over there?" His breath was hot on Jason's face and Jason was relieved to see that Adam was sweating. Perhaps he had had enough as well.

"In the upper drawer," Jason told him. "There might be more cash in there."

Adam grinned cruelly. "That's better." He pushed Jason toward the desk.

Standing in full view of the window Jason pulled the door open and dug through the contents. Adam stood close behind him with his arms folded.

"Maybe in another drawer…" Jason muttered bending to open the next one.

"If this is a trick…"

There was muffled crack and Adam's voice caught strangely in his throat. Jason glanced up in time to see the shocked look in his attacker's eyes fade into a dull unseeing stare as the man crumpled silently to the ground.

Jason did not move, he did not have to, Adam was dead. Jason turned back to the window. A small circular hole in the screen caught his eye.

Jason wondered briefly why it took the sniper so long to make the shot, but the thought was gone as soon as it had come. Walking gingerly around the body, Jason made his way to the stairs. He sat, a bit shakily and waited. He could hear sirens in the distance and somehow he knew they were coming for him.

He did not have long to wait. Three police cars, parked at an angle to shield their drivers filled the yard with their strobing lights.

The light pulsed in through the open window in the room above where Jason sat, but he was too weary to rise. Jason had done some thinking while he was being tossed around by Adam, and more while he waited on the step. He could do everything in his power to protect those he loved, but like Ellen had said, the only real protection came from the Lord. With a barely audible prayer, Jason once again gave his family into the care of the Lord. Jason was their protector as a father and husband, but the tense fearful way he had been living was evidence of his lack of trust in the Lord.

"Come out with your hands up," Graham shouted. He had the perfect commanding voice, Jason mused.

"This is Jason Roper. It's all clear." Jason noticed his own voice was a bit unsteady. He heard the cautious tread of feet as the officers approached the garage, weapons ready.

"Are you alright?" It was Mike's voice this time.

"He's dead," he informed them dully.

They entered cautiously, ready for an attack.

Jason understood; it was the perfect setup for an attack. "He really is dead," Jason told them.

"Are you alright?" Mike asked again, concern written on his face.

"You know me," Jason joked halfheartedly.

Mike grinned and pressed the radio on his shoulder. "All clear, I have secured the hostage." Mike looked up at Jason who was still seated on the stairs. "How did it happen?"

"Yeah," Graham joined Mike at the bottom of the steps. "We got a strange call about some guy being run over tonight. The news came out and everything and the guy was gone." As Graham spoke, several police investigators hurried up the steps to evaluate the room and deal with Adam's body.

"Even the ambulance," Graham continued, "that allegedly took him to the hospital, arrived empty with no word of explanation. The news is going crazy over it. All they have is a bad video of the hit and run from someone's cell phone."

Mike exchanged a knowing look with Jason.

Graham went on, unaware. "So that guy gets run over and vanishes and then someone gave us an anonymous tip that you were being held here." Graham shook his head. "It has been a strange night."

Jason smiled a little. Eddie's forethought was, as always, flawless. "It has been a long night for us all," Jason observed.

"Mike, come up here," an officer called.

Jason appreciated the light hand on his shoulder as Mike passed. "Graham, would you mind taking me home?"

———

Mike paused at the top of the stairs. The scene had already been captured on camera and the body was being loaded onto a stretcher to be taken away. Mike surveyed the room, the place was a wreck. The chair had been smashed, the bed covers partially torn from the bed, the table lay on its side and the pictures had been knocked from the walls. Picking his way across the room he made his way to the officer waiting by the window.

"Jason didn't kill this man," the officer pointed out. "The dead man had a few indents in his bullet proof vest, but that," he gestured to the screened window, "is the shot that killed him."

Mike gently touched the circular hole in the screen. "A sniper?"

"Looks like it," the officer agreed. "I radioed it in and got word from the search party in the house."

"What did they say?" Mike asked taking his eyes from the window.

"The house was completely empty except for two papers lying beside the upstairs window. One was a copy of the warrant for the dead man's arrest, and the second a letter of assignment from a special agent on the federal level. We can only assume he is the one who fired the deadly shot."

NINETEEN

"How did you get the house so fast?" Jason asked. He was sitting on the couch with an arm around Ellen. It had been a long and trying night for all of them, but no one felt like sleeping. "The house was all made up, just like a movie set,"

Eddie shrugged. "I have connections."

"Yes, but to buy a house and a car and set it all up…Eddie I'm seriously impressed." Jason glanced at Ellen. "And I don't know how I can ever repay you."

"Friends don't have to repay, Roper," Eddie informed him. "Friends are just there for each other. You would have done the same for me."

"So they are all behind bars?" Ellen asked.

"Or under the ground," Benjamin interjected. "Eddie got the last man."

"It wasn't me," Eddie corrected. "I was here all night. I got a friend who specializes in sniping. I don't know anyone better." Eddie rose from his chair. "If you need me, Benjamin has my number."

"You're leaving?" Ellen asked. "You just got here."

"I did what I came for, Miss Ellen. Now I'll get out of your way. I guess you have some packing to do?"

Jason rose and shook Eddie's hand. "I'll try to get your gun back once this blows over."

"You can have it, for a keep sake." Eddie grinned. "I have a few more stashed away."

"It was good to see you again, Eddie. Thank you for coming."

Benjamin stood and offered his splinted hand. Eddie shook it gently. "Thanks for calling me, Benjamin. Take care of that foot."

"I will," Benjamin answered. "Thanks for your help."

Eddie went to the door and did a quick check before stepping out into the darkness. A sleek black car was waiting by the curb.

"Take care of yourself, Eddie. Thanks again."

"I wouldn't mind if you left me out of your statement to the cops," Eddie informed Jason confidentially.

Jason pretended to be surprised. "You mean you were involved?"

Eddie laughed and slapped Jason on the shoulder. "Not in the slightest." He strolled easily across the lawn and walked around to the driver's door. Pulling it open he waved once more before sliding inside.

Jason lifted his hand in farewell as the car pulled away and headed down the street.

He was still standing there when a police cruiser pulled up and parked where Eddie's car had been. Mike got out and came up to where Jason stood in the glow of the porch light.

"Hey Mike. Did they get it all sorted out?"

Mike shook his head. "All I can say, is that you have some serious explaining to do."

Jason laughed. "Don't worry, I'll think of something."

———

"Peter Farley, I find you guilty of soliciting to commit murder, attempted kidnapping, soliciting to commit larceny, engaging a minor in criminal activities and possession and trafficking of an illegal substance. I sentence you to life plus 120 years without parole." The judge's gavel rapped on the desk and the room buzzed as Farley, handcuffed and dressed in an orange jumpsuit, was led out of the courtroom.

Jason and Mike left the court room quickly while the press swarmed around Farley for pictures.

Once they were in the car Jason sighed. "Well that's over."

"And on to moving," Mike announced pulling into traffic.

They rode in silence for a while before Mike spoke up. "I'm going to miss you, Jason. You have been a great partner."

"You were the best." Jason smiled sadly watching the scenery go by. "I'm sorry it has to end this way."

More time passed in silence.

"I've got something for you." Jason pulled a worn book from his duffle bag.

"Yeah?" Mike glanced over at the book in Jason's hand. "What is it?"

"It's my duty Bible." Jason ran his hand lovingly over the worn cover.

"What does that mean?"

"It is the one I kept in my cruiser. The one I carried in my duffle."

"With your extra cover up clothes?" Mike asked with a grin.

Jason gave him a little shove. "I couldn't exactly come walking up to the chief with bullet holes in my clothes."

Mike was still grinning.

"Anyway," Jason said after a minute. "I want you to have it. I marked in it some over the years, I hope you don't mind. Kind of something to remember me by."

"How could I forget the only invincible person I've ever met?" Mike asked. "I still can't believe you got away with it for three years."

Jason looked down at the Bible on his lap. "I just wish it could have been longer."

———

"I got something to tell you," Seth blurted out, interrupting Benjamin mid-sentence. They had almost used up all the allotted counseling time, and Seth did not want to leave without saying his piece.

Benjamin waited expectantly. His black eye had faded to a grayish yellow and a pair of crutches leaned against the table beside him.

"You know that little Bible you gave me a while back?"

"The one you said you would throw away?" Benjamin asked with a sparkle.

Seth was embarrassed. "Yeah, well I didn't. I got to reading it. Especially the little I John book."

The edges of Benjamin's mouth twitched but he managed to suppress the smile before it showed through.

"Well, I was thinking about it all. How God gave His Son for sin and stuff. I don't know if I did it right, but I told God I believed what He did."

Benjamin brightened and a grin spread across his face.

"Do you think He can forgive me like He forgives all those good people who do all the right stuff? I read somewhere about a thief who was being executed with Jesus. God still forgave him, so I thought I might have a chance."

"Seth, God says that whoever believes on the name of the Lord will be saved. But that's not where it stops. You have to repent. Which means to turn away from your sin and go the other way."

"Like toward God?" Seth asked.

"Yeah, to do what He says instead of what you want or you are used to doing," Benjamin answered.

"How do I know what He says?" Seth asked.

"Keep reading the Bible," Benjamin replied. "You read about loving people in first John didn't you?"

"Yeah."

"So start there. If you stay in God's word, He'll teach you. I've got to leave after one more visit, but I'll give you my number." Benjamin scribbled it down on the corner of his paper, tore it off, and handed it to Seth. "You can call me collect and I'll try to help you work through the tough parts. I don't know everything but we can look it up together."

Seth looked down at the number. "That'd be cool."

———

Jason pulled the door of the moving truck closed and locked it into place. Everything was packed away safely inside. Benjamin had brought his family to help them with the packing. They had pulled out and headed for home early that morning.

"All aboard," Jason called loudly.

Ellen came out of the house juggling Levi and the diaper bag. Jason took Levi and strapped him into his seat. "Be a good boy for Mommy." Jason handed him a toy and went around to start the car.

"Kara?" Ellen called "Where are you?"

"She's in the truck with Benj," Jason told her. "Do you mind if I take them for the first shift? I thought Levi might sleep better that way."

"Yes, that's fine. They will have fun while the trip is still new." Ellen looked back at the house. "This was a good little house."

"Yeah, I'm going to miss it." Jason went to stand by her and put his arm around her waist.

"Did you get a chance to say goodbye to Mike?"

"I stopped by the station this morning and formally retired from the force."

"I bet they were sad to see you go."

"It helped that they had the month's notice." Jason looked the house over one last time.

"Daddy, are we leaving yet?" Benj called from the cab of the truck.

Jason laughed and looked down at Ellen. "Are you ready?"

She smiled and nodded.

"Let's go."

STRENGTH OF SILENCE

Eddie stayed where he was, listening. In the distance, a motor started up. He waited until it had faded before he stood. Dizziness washed over him, and he steadied himself against the counter. Still moving unsteadily, Eddie removed the floorboards and laid them aside. He heard something out front and froze. If the police caught him here, there would be no end of trouble. Moving toward the back door Eddie pushed it open. Outside, trash cans and a variety of other things littered the yard. A car motor rumbled toward him, and Eddie ran.

JASON ROPER

Infused with invincibility and trained for greatness, Jason Roper is set to fulfill his father's dreams. But when Roper deviates from the instructions he is given, he stumbles upon an expansive criminal network. Determined to use his power to help those in need, Jason Roper discovers that there are times when invincibility alone is not enough.

Is Jason Roper destined for greatness as he has been told, or is his life just a front for a larger, more sinister plan?

Roper Returns

Jason Roper's second mission is clear-cut. He moves in with confidence, feeling invincible and unstoppable. But things are not what they appear on the surface. Even his invincibility has limits Roper did not know.

With no one to turn to, Roper finds himself sinking into a darkness he does not have the power to evade.

The Man Behind The Melody

The unexpected death of his twin sister threw Mark into a whirlwind of change. Disowned by his stepfather, Mark set out with only one goal in mind, to get as far away from the hateful man as possible. He clung desperately to the last link with his sister, her saxophone. Wandering the streets, Mark's path crossed with a stranger who could see potential no one else could see. Mark, an unwanted orphan, was offered the chance to become more than he had ever dreamed. But could the stranger be trusted?

Carbon
An Unforgettable Adventure

Carbon slipped out of bed and turned on the light. Taking a sheet of thick drawing paper from her desk she drew the face of the man the article simply called Roper. Pulling the picture she had drawn earlier from her file box, she laid them side by side on the desk. It was little or nothing to go on. The prisoner could have been a thousand different people. She had no face to compare. Suddenly the image of the stranger in the alley came to mind and Carbon frowned thoughtfully. He was the only one who would know.

Taken by the Deep

"Must be a storm." Jeremy tried to sound confident.

"It's not a storm, Jeremy." Lydia's face was white and her voice faded into a whisper. "Please, you've got to let me go."

They didn't seem to hear her. Their eyes were riveted on the swirling water before them. It rose slowly as if the waves were standing, then moved forward with hypnotic swiftness.

Lydia screamed as the waters dove toward them. The salty spray wrapped around her, wrenching her from their grasp and pulling her into its depth.

In Visible Fear

Billy dropped back on the bed, flickering between the visible world and the invisible. His breathing was rapid and irregular.

"Keep quiet, Billy, and I'll do my best to keep them off your trail. They were asking about you today."

"Don't let them find me." Again, Billy grasped the man's shirt, terror in his eyes.

The dark man pried his fingers open and stepped away. "You keep your mouth shut, I'll do what I can."

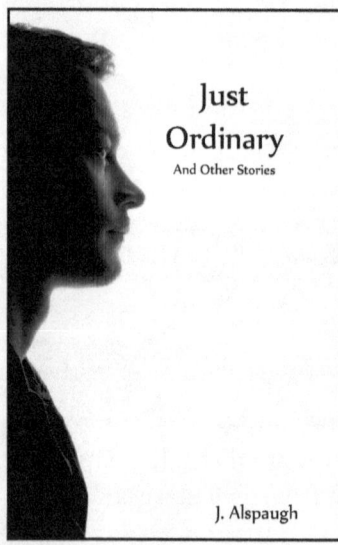

Just Ordinary
And Other Stories

Is there anyone who is truly just ordinary? Step into the world of fiction where heroes face mythical enemies, wrestle against enticing deceit, and battle fierce storms in a struggle for life. Experience heartbreak, adventure, and the ultimate sacrifice as you delve into the stories of *Just Ordinary*.

THE STRIKER OF CHOI

The health of the Striker is the health of Choi. If he goes hungry, the town of Choi will grow hungry. If he is injured, the townspeople will suffer injury. He must be protected at all costs and must never leave the town of his birth. If he were to leave, the curse of the town would be in the hands of strangers.

Striker knew the legend well, but was there more to the legend than he had been told?

THE SWORD OF JUSTICE

His mission was to eliminate those who had received the death penalty from the king. Justice was a King's Man. A man who had sworn allegiance to the king and who was backed in power by the full authority of the king himself. A man hated by every criminal in the king's realm.

Would Justice's loyalty to the king and skill with a sword be enough to protect him from his enemies?